KING
TITAN

KING TITAN

ADLAI E. MACK

XULON PRESS

Xulon Press
2301 Lucien Way #415
Maitland, FL 32751
407.339.4217
www.xulonpress.com

Paperback ISBN-13: 978-1-66287-000-2
Ebook ISBN-13: 978-1-66287-001-9

This book is dedicated to my wife, Sandra.

Table of Contents

Preface

This is Christian fiction, a giant monster story. However, the history of the world is replete with terrors, such as the thunder lizards, the swamps of Zaire from which natives flee, and the reports of sea-faring Vikings that saw their ships pulled under by giant octopuses. Many Biblical accounts describe monsters that leaves one breathless: most notably Leviathan, Jonah's whale and Behemoth. Other Biblical creatures are included in the appendix of this book.

The author's focus is not the fear that these monsters evoke, but how they can move humanity to turn to God, who changes people's behaviors and their beliefs. Jonah's whale was in this tradition.

Adlai E. Mack, Christmastide 2022

CHAPTER 1

ROMANCE

Meet Ed and Mary, who found true love with each other and with God.

Ed Blackstone was the submarine's Chief. He was like a father-figure to the crew, to the non-officers. He showed them basic living skills, like how to make their beds, shine their shoes, hang up their clothes, and how to write a letter of thanks. He trained them to manage their finances and pay their bills on time. He taught them to show respect to their elders, and to attend church faithfully. Although still a bachelor, he also talked to the young men about obtaining, treating, and keeping a good wife. They had lots of questions! Most sailors were insecure, fearful, 18-year-old boys who were now experiencing their first time away from home. Ed was the available, patient and fun, but firm, role model many of them never had at home. He was tall, strong, and handsome, and a former basketball player, although he could play anything with a ball. Through the influence of his Captain, mentor and father in the Christian faith, Joe Davis, Ed had become a true man of faith.

Chief Ed Blackstone was long in coming to a marrying mood. In his younger life, like so many others, he did not value the relationship between sex, romance and marriage. But now, Ed wanted to settle down. He had the right woman this time, and his heart had been transformed by his Christian faith. Mary was everything he ever wanted in a wife.

They met when Mary returned a lost dog to its owner, a Christian friend of Mary's named Joe Davis. He was with Ed at the time, and introduced him as "Chief" and a very good friend of his. Joe's dog was a rare blue male Great Dane named Caesar. He was so excited to be returned home, that he sideswiped Ed and knocked him to the ground! As he got up, he and Mary exchanged a concise, embarrassed, "Hi!" As their eyes met, Ed almost fell over again! This was the woman he had seen at age 12 in a night vision, very accurately, while asleep: a tall, white, red-haired beauty, who loved God, and her name was revealed in the vision as Mary! On the strength of that word, he had courted many women while looking for her.

At first, Ed was hindered from dating Mary by being in a dead-end relationship with another woman. When they broke up, he began seeing Mary. Over the next few months, Mary met most of Ed's friends. She thought it was remarkable that she liked them too.

Now, Ed could pursue a vision of holiness whole-heartedly and build a wholesome life. He was on a search for excellence in all his pursuits, which he learned from the Bible, his friends and, most recently, from Mary.

Mary remarked later that, when she first was introduced to him by Joe, a great peace came over her. She felt safe with him, and totally respected and appreciated. Their first date was to go to church together. She noticed that he wasn't putting his hands all over her, and he put no pressure on her to have sex. He very early on said, "Jesus all the way. No sex until marriage, and once married, only sex with one's spouse." He said, "Joe Davis helped me to see that and be unswerving in that commitment."

His closest friends on the submarine were the Captain, Joe Davis; McKinley, a high-ranking lieutenant; Craig Stevens, the boat's EXO; John Anderson, a nerd who was called the Brainiac (he was the ship's computer whiz, a degree-holding mechanical engineer who had made a name for himself in his late 20's;) Chui Hernandez, a master code breaker; Enoch Chang, weapons expert and martial arts master; Running Bear, a linguist; George Clark, communications man and peacemaker; and Jeffrey Brown, who was the best sonar man in the navy. Besides them, their pastor was Chaplain Gaines, and his slightly younger assistant, a mature officer, whom they all affectionately called "The Preacher," who aspired to be a Bishop and a pastor of a church when his term of service was over.

Many fellow sailors on the base jokingly called these friends the "Holy Club." Others called them the "Detroit Submarine Saints," or just "the saints." Some were averse to the word "saint" being applied to them, for they weren't sinless, not even close. But they attempted to grow into the term because it was Biblical and historical, and was applied to first century Christians like St. Peter, St. Paul, and St. Mary, who had faults and struggled in the flesh on earth. This fellowship of submariners still had slips into unholy acts. But the word "holy" kept them challenged with a better vision for themselves at all times.

So they were a holy club, saints, a rare group to be sure. And they were making a lifelong, rocky, arduous climb together, from a very low spot in morals, doctrine, life history, and the knowledge of God, till they reached the 'Mountain Top' and saw the 'Lights of Glory.' They didn't mind the climb. It was an adventure since Jesus was with them and they had one another to make the trip more enjoyable, more like teamwork. And they didn't mind being rare. That made them more valuable!

How did this holy club work out in practice on a busy submarine? Chaplain Gaines taught them to keep prayer times short but disciplined. Sometimes they could do brief prayers together at daybreak, like read a Psalm, recite the Lord's Prayer and perhaps sing a hymn. On other days, they could do both morning and noon prayers. On a smooth day, they might fit in three prayer times, the third at day's end, and usually the shortest of all. When they couldn't get together, they did as many of these prayer times alone as possible.

Mary Braswell was Ed's dream girl that he had searched so hard for since he was a boy of 12 years old. Mary had been home-schooled. She had earned her Bachelor of Science degree in Physics at a Christian University and was well established as a naval officer and aviator. She loved camping, hiking and everything outdoors. She was also an animal lover. She was tall, lean, red-headed, long-limbed, and had long hair and a smile that would make a man's head swim. She was also strong, and superb in volleyball and no slouch in self-defense either. But she was also gentle of speech, kind, and patient. Mary's extended family had a regular prayer group, which met in their country home for many years, in the solace of Grass Lake, California. Its founder, visionary and intercessor was Mary's grandfather, Charles Braswell. The group was known to have great power and insight in prayer. Each person shared their spiritual gifts in this holy club: readers, singers, theologians, historians, visionaries, missionaries, intercessors and so on. Mary was privileged to grow up in this on a weekly basis, from being a baby-in-arms to becoming a strong woman of God. The combined wisdom of three generations of faithful Bible observance created a godly vision of courtship and marriage for Mary to emulate. Her grandmother often said, "Having strong courtships, marriages, and families is like training for the Olympics. Only those who follow strict paths obtain the gold or win the medals." Mary took this to heart, and made a vow to God as a young woman to remain a virgin until her wedding night. And with that commitment firmly made, she focused on improving herself by learning wisdom and skills. She developed herself inwardly and outwardly to become an excellent naval pilot, good friend and great cook. She avoided drugs, alcohol and tobacco.

Mary and her family were part of a backlash, a holiness revival that Jesus was doing on earth. Her spirituality was intensely practical and domestic, like her mom's and grandmother's. She loved church and loved to dress modestly. She learned from older, wiser folks who gave her good counsel on holy living, friendships, finances, possessions, politics, role models and almost every other practical aspect of life. She loved to read Christian classics, and rarely watched TV. Mary clearly took the "way less travelled," but with more admirers and adherents than she could know or think.

Mary was strong, but not without feelings and wounds, nor beyond fear. The morning before her engagement, she read about Naomi in the Bible, who became bitter, lonely, and bereaved, without a husband, sons or daughters, except Ruth. Naomi was so bitter, she changed her name to "Mara," meaning bitter. (Mary, too, can mean 'bitter' as a derivative of 'Mara.') She also had a bitter side. She could be melancholy and she seriously wondered if she would ever get married. Would Ed pop the question to her, or would he wed some other beautiful girl, while she would grow old, gray, fat and lonely? But even if she never married, Mary had promised God that she would love the Lord Jesus, and serve Him with all she had. It seemed God liked that prayer, and that attitude!

Ed, however, was not so blessed with an ideal family background and past. His parents had divorced when he was twelve years old. They started out well. Ed had happy memories of attending church, reading the Bible, family vacations in the country and growing a vegetable garden when he was a small child. But when they stopped all that, his dad became violent and his mom was cold-hearted, and they spread a lot of sorrow everywhere. He used to hide in his bedroom and lock his door as Mom and Dad were screaming, cussing, breaking things, and fighting. Eventually the family broke up. He blamed himself for their divorce, as many children do. He unfortunately developed a lot of anger and bitterness himself which took years to conquer. He was angry at both his mom and his dad for forsaking him and their pet dog. His two heroes had failed him, and abandoned the life that made him proud of them. Once he was in Christ, he forgave them both and spent quality time with them. But he made a vow never to do marriage or family that way, but God's way, when he met the right girl. Years after that terrible rending of their family, his parents both returned to God. They became strong practicing Christians, and forgave each other and reconciled, and remarried each other. But nonetheless, the damage had already been done in Ed's life.

Unlike Mary's godly commitments, Ed's experience was full of slips over the years with the opposite sex. He had some irresponsible, selfish and mostly loveless, unmarried relationships, all with tall redheads. They left him hurt and feeling dirty, and sometimes sick as well. Living with them unmarried was the most abusive and dishonest thing he ever did. In fact, he got a nickname in his worldly days of "The Redhead

Player,' a memory that later caused him much shame. Those women played him, too; they played sweet Ed for all he was worth. They were named Mary or similar names such as Marilyn and Marianne. But they were not his intended Mary. After meeting the real Mary, Ed prayed hard that God would forgive him, save him, deliver him and give him a new heart. If He did, he'd go "the whole nine yards" with Jesus, with strict Christian courtship, marriage and family life. He also confessed his sins to a Reverend, and asked him to pray a prayer of deliverance over him. It worked. God gave him his wish, a whole new start on life and another chance to make it work. This time, living the Bible way, he would exceed his parents' achievements, avoid their failures, and create a whole new line of marriage and family success.

The day they became engaged, Ed visited Mary at work. She was in her work scrubs. Ed came to the secretary, and asked if he could see Mary Braswell, or "tall Mary" as the short lady called her.

She replied, "Sure thing!" She called Mary on the loudspeaker. "Mary Braswell, you have a visitor at the front desk." So she headed that way.

As soon as Ed saw her, he shouted her name excitedly. "Mary!" It was as if he hadn't seen his best friend in 20 years! He then ran toward her. Before she knew it, she was running toward him too, with tears of joy running down her face! The body language was unmistakable to her. It was a big surprise, and this was her big day! Their big day! She knew it! They caught and embraced one another in the air, spinning each other around!

She grasped him like a wrestler, crying, "My love! My love!"

And he, in a standing bear hug, said, "Will you be mine? Will you be mine? I love you so very much!"

They both kept saying, "Yes! Yes! Yes! I'll marry you!"

Both Ed and Mary were people of their word. They were engaged to be married "until death do us part." That night Ed took Mary to buy her a gorgeous engagement and wedding ring pair. Ed promised to wed Mary in a country church, as soon as his next submarine tour was over. And she promised the same to him.

As the submarine was being serviced in San Diego harbor, Ed and Mary took advantage of this leave and visited the home where she grew up in Grass Lake, California; a beautiful, forested, mountain location with four seasons. There was a wide running stream, the noisy kind with water crashing into rocks, especially after a heavy rain. They wanted to buy a modest house where they could start a family. Their dads were helping to fulfill that dream for them.

Mary planned to cease her military career after they had children and be a stay-at-home mom. She wanted to nurture her children, do Christian home-schooling, and raise farm animals. That is, "if God wills." That became their bed-rock phrase.

A few days before the submarine deployment, the holy club sponsored a party. Jeffrey brought Brenda to it; it was her first Christian party. Before this year, all such things seemed to her as a dull, boring exercise in phoniness and dark funeral clothes. She thought only LA night clubs knew how to party. The Pastor was there along with his wife. It began in prayer, and then introductions. Everyone had a nametag and was pleasantly dressed in a variety of attractive colors and was friendly. Many ethnic groups were present, including Black and White, Haitian, Asian, Latino, African, Samoan, and Indian! They served a full course Mexican food dinner, for which San Diego was famous. It was a hit! So were the homemade lemonade, iced tea, punch and apple pie! Mary made the apple pie and Ed made the iced tea. Besides this, they played several group games together, and gave out prizes to the winners, with much laughter and enthusiastic loud talking and cheering! Brenda remarked to herself that this was her best party ever. There was no drunkenness, no fighting, no cussing, no half-naked people, no drugs, no dirty jokes, no seductive music, and no one taking out someone else's spouse. Just totally wholesome and non-racist. She felt very comfortable and accepted.

Following the party, Jeffrey drove Brenda to her apartment said, "I'm tired, and I'm going home to get a good night's sleep at a decent hour."

Brenda replied, "It's only 9 p.m.! Come in! We've never been intimate yet, just holding hands, and hugs, and I love you. You know that I go to church and I believe in Jesus as my personal Savior, but we don't have to be fanatics. For God's sake, it's Friday night, and most of the girls I know, both inside and outside the church, spend this night sleeping with their boyfriends."

Jeffrey responded, "No! No! No! I want a godly wife. If it was really 'for God's sake,' your girlfriends would obey the Bible and keep their clothes on and not fornicate. And if it was really love that they are expressing - it sounds like lust to me - then they would wait for their wedding day, and they would help each other draw near to God and be ready for Heaven. They would serve God together and protect each other from sin, Satan, and Hell. What do you want? True love that's faithful to you while we're apart? Or mere physical love, so that if you deny me tonight, I'll be with a different woman tomorrow. Which?"

Brenda felt blessed and loved by Jeffrey and God, and was actually proud of Jeff despite her protests. She could hardly keep back her smile of admiration.

Jeffrey continued. "There's a difference between you and me. You think God is exaggerating or kidding when He speaks of sending people to Hell, that He couldn't be that strict. But He is. You should read Luke 19:21-22 and

Deuteronomy 22. Why, it's so plain a blind man can see it. No sex 'til marriage or outside of it. In Matthew 25:24, He calls Himself hard and austere as His own self-description, which means strict. I believe He's totally serious, totally strict. Yes, and totally loving." Jeffrey wanted to run away from her right then.

Brenda offered, "Well, if we can't make love, how about going with me to the night club to dance the night away and have a few drinks? They have some great barbecue ribs!"

Jeffrey frowned. "I gave up that loud, vulgar, overly sexed, ear-splitting noise when I got saved. The typical club with lots of half-naked girls and guys, trying to woo the men or the women, or both, is not for me. My speed now is gospel hymns and anthems, some classical, folk, and Celtic music. I'm starting to think that we need to go our separate ways and break up."

Brenda, bursting into tears, cried, "Oh no! Not so drastic. You're the first decent, trustworthy, God-honoring man I've ever had. You make me a better person. That's what I really want. I am getting a lot closer to Christ with you. Give me another chance to redo this discussion and this night. Let's just close this night with a short prayer so I can let you get your sleep at home. Will you write me every week?"

Jeffrey sighed, "I'll do my best."

"I will respond to every letter with true love. I respect you, and I will respect your, now our, mutual purity commitment. Pray for me. One thing you know, I'm not a liar. I keep my word," Brenda said with a smile.

Jeffrey smiled back. "Yes, you do."

Those last two weeks, Ed and Mary prayed and read together a lot. They spent their break happily riding bikes on forest roads and to the beaches; having long, pleasant talks and walks in the park; sitting together in fragrant flower gardens; rowing on beautiful Grass Lake under a full moon; speed boating in San Diego harbor; swimming in an Olympic-sized pool; and enjoying moonlight dinners at San Diego's finest restaurants. One day, they drove further to hike and picnic in the world-famous, supremely gorgeous Paradise mountains. They were inseparable, like two peas in a pod. They did everything together, church and everything! They had such great fun and blissful memories of this leave together. They only left one big thing out (according to this world's current "wisdom,") and that was sex. Their worldly contacts told them they should "try each other out first," to see if they will like each other, or if the two would be compatible sexually. To counter, Ed would respond, "Fresher is better. That practice only confuses loyalties and thoughts. It creates flashbacks to previous lovers, inhibits fidelity, fosters guilt, cheapens each other, and eventually leads to Hell." He would know. Besides, they were happy without it. They were totally committed to wait until after they took their official wedding vows, and gave each other something far more Biblical and loving than sweet nothings, empty promises, a condom, the pill, or an abortifacient.

Ed's wallet was now empty, after having so much fun with Mary. But from that point on, they would be thrifty and disciplined with finances, too.

Ed had no regrets this time. He and Mary set a firm agreed-upon vision as a couple to "cross every 'T' and dot every 'I.'" He would say, "We will follow every word of God's good Book, the old-fashioned King James Holy Bible. Old-fashioned is 'fine and dandy' for us. God knew from the beginning what to say to us and how to say it, so He did in the Bible: God's written, officially notarized Scripture."

Mary would joke, "I'm so conservative, the evening news wants to censor me!" She would break out laughing, so pretty-like. They were very excited about their mutual vision to follow the old time-tested KJV Bible as a couple, and as a family eventually, if God willed to bless them with children. What an adventure they were on together!

Mary made a last call to Ed, asking their mutual friend Joe Davis, who was with him at the dock, could she please speak to "Lover Boy." With a big smile and a chuckle, he said, "Phone call, for lover boy!" Ed took the phone, and Joe could hardly get them to stop talking.

Her last words to him were, "Write or call me, and try to share a Scripture with me as often as you can, and don't forget to tell me why it was special to you at the time. Stay with your chaplain; he has a good word. Maintain your prayers. Go to church, my love. Save the world! I love you, and I can't wait till we are in each other's arms again. Let us both remember God's promise in Psalm 84.11, 'No good thing will He withhold from them that walk uprightly.'"

As they were about to board the submarine, Ed replied, "Missing you already, love of my life. I love you!"

Mary said sweetly, "Stay in touch!"

"I will!" Ed assured her. "Don't worry, I've got my buddies, McKinley, John, Craig, Joe, George, Enoch and Chui, Running Bear, and Jeffrey to help me stand strong with God; plus, I've got Jesus. Better than that, He has me, really and truly! Our Blackstone goal is 'great likeness to Jesus.' As such, we are awesome weapons in the hands of God."

"After this trip, the next one will be our honeymoon!" Mary said excitedly.

The tug boat came to tow the submarine out of the harbor and into the wide and blue Pacific Ocean. It did so with Captain Joe Davis, the EXO Craig Stevens, and Chief Ed standing on top, on the "sail" as it's called, waving goodbye to San Diego with its ideal climate, and to those still standing on the dock in San Diego Harbor, waving back: moms, dads, siblings, spouses, friends, and relatives. It was quite a crowd, at least for them. The ocean was calm and the air breezy and warm. Fishing birds were diving into the ocean and coming up with a healthy catch. They had a strange mixture of feelings of longing to stay here, of missing loved ones, of patriotism and of courage. They were somehow excited, but nervous. They said, "It's the job, so you do your very best to the Glory of God."

Their orders were sealed, and they were not to open them until they arrived in the Indian Ocean. Why so urgent a leaving to the hot Indian Ocean? The submariners speculated that it would be "a very dangerous tour," "shrouded in dark mystery," "a dreadful one," and "a lonely scraping of the bottom of the ocean inside a moving bomb called a sub."

Truth be told, most were very worried, both on land and now at sea.

CHAPTER 2

SUBMARINE INTRIGUE

They were told to make all speed. The Rear
Admiral gave Captain Joe Davis a communication to head
straight for the Indian Ocean where they will rendezvous
with "the Black, the Formidable, the Gigantic." He was told,
"You'll know it when you see it." The Captain related the command to the EXO, Craig Stevens, and he to the Chief, Ed
Blackstone. The three related the orders to the crew. Those
were all the clues they were given as they navigated the many
waters. Not even the President of the United States or the
Navy higher-ups knew exactly what those words meant.

Ed and his buddies all took a knee to ask God for a safe
trip. They thanked Him for good families and a quiet depar-
ture from San Diego and the USA. They expressed grati-
tude that they lived in a land of jobs and opportunity. The
Captain commanded to engage their nuclear-powered engine
and life support systems, look the part, look sharp, look alive,
close the hatch, submerge to 300-feet deep, and move with all
speed to the Indian Ocean, where they will confront the great

unknown, or this thing called "the Black, the Formidable, the Gigantic."

The USS *Detroit*, a Los Angeles Class Attack Submarine, was a combat vessel of the United States Navy, designed to chase, catch, and attack enemy ships and submarines and to quickly destroy them. It was about 350-feet long, carried about 134 crew members, including officers, and was nuclear powered. It had central air that could last many months at a time under water. It was fully equipped with sonar, radar, GPS, radio, television, and a periscope. The USS *Detroit* had a satellite link, as well as Sea-Scan, an underwater torpedo-shaped drone with a camera and high beam headlight, giving the submarine clear pictures in dark waters. It carried guided torpedoes and short range nuclear ballistic missiles, which could be launched through four torpedo tubes. It also had twelve vertical launch tubes in the bow for cruise missiles. It was propeller driven, had a "sail" on top, which was all strong metal, and had two large wings on it to raise or lower the sub's depth. From the sail, the captain could look through its periscope, 360 degrees. The USS *Detroit* had an inner and outer hull to deal with extreme water pressures. There were close working quarters in every room with multiple men working in each area. A mini-submarine, that could get to them from anywhere in the world, could dock on top of the USS *Detroit*.

Its' commander at present was Captain Joe Davis, a graduate of Annapolis. He attended a Christian College for a few years, like his pop, but decided that he was more suited to a military career. Davis was incredibly well-read with a distinguished record. He was also an experienced Renaissance man, commander and captain. He was the "cream of the crop."

Captain hollered, "Do a last check on all weapons systems." Everything passed with flying colors. The engines were purring like a kitten.

About two weeks later, the submarine was descending at six degrees and making revolutions of her propeller at 20 knots, descending to a depth of 800 feet. Sea-Scan, an underwater drone, was lighting the way in the dark waters and filming excellent pictures. A mini-submarine had docked on top of the hull late that night. Navy SEALs were expecting to carry out a special mission with it when they arrived near the Port of Diego Garcia in the Indian Ocean.

It was just moments after sunrise on a Sunday morning. The Christian officers, called the "Holy Club" and several seamen had just finished a short early morning prayer meeting on the sub. The Chaplain was present and his assistant. So was Chief Ed, John, Jeffrey, and the EXO, and McKinley, Chui and Enoch, Running Bear, and George Clark. The Captain felt uneasy in his spirit that morning. In fact, he was very troubled for some yet-unknown reason. The sea life seemed equally disturbed, in their pageant of colors and beautiful migrations, as many millions of them stepped aside, moving all at the same time in the waters. The question was, "Why?"

As there was nothing on their itinerary, most of the USS *Detroit* submarine crew were expecting a boring day. The crew was jovial, noisy, and teasing one another roughly, as men do, and was a little too happy-go-lucky, talking smack and shop talk. Seaman Willie Jones had just arrived in the torpedo room in the front part of the inner sub. He was a Black, inner-city man from the projects, and a Southerner who had graduated with honors from high school. He said to E-van Roberts, father of Angelo and Emily Roberts, loud and teasing, "E-van-der Holyfield! What's happening, man? I mean, what's coming down? How does it feel to be the heavy weight boxing world champion? Cool, I bet! Did you get that ear fixed? It looks good! What are your plans for Mike Tyson? The real deal is, this is your day! You can count on that; it's your week! Because Willie is in town—I mean in the *house*, baby! The king is here, and your problems are going to be solved! What you got for me today? I suspect we'll fire some torpedoes, baby, like warriors, and chop it up, as the inception of war, to defend the USA and our allies, or something more personal, to take out those who attack this sub, submariners, our children, and our sweethearts, and watch those guided water missiles blow bad folks away!" He made an exploding noise with his tongue, with a big, confident smile and pretty white teeth.

"Quiet!" Officer Jeffrey Brown, the sonar technician, gestured with his hand in the air. His head was tilted and he was very, very focused, doing all his checks. He was captured by the screen in front of him and the size of the moving object on the sonar. There were unusual sounds emanating from it.

"Quiet!" Captain spoke over the loud speaker.

Captain said calmly, "EXO has the Con." Then, sharply, "I don't want to hear a whisper! You hear me? We don't want to spook this thing."

McKinley nodded. "Aye, Captain." Then over the loud speaker, he commanded, "Condition ultra-quiet."

Their alarm got the attention of others and all were immediately silent. None dared drop a dish or a spoon in the USS *Detroit* for about 20 minutes. They used the quiet period to check all their instruments and make sure everything worked properly. Officer Jeffrey Brown was doing all his checks to build a picture of the moving object on the sonar.

Ed pulled out a beautiful picture of Mary, which he kept with him, to inspire him to do his best, and to come back alive from this trip. He wanted to finally obtain his long-sought-after prize. Other men on the boat were doing similarly with pictures they had. Many included children. One man, a fine artist, had a hand-drawn sketch of his sweetheart that gave him strength, hope and resolve to stay alive.

Captain sternly ordered, "Recall Sea-Scan. As soon as it returns, make your coordinates four degrees down, moving northeast, speed 20 knots, course, come right 150—"

He was interrupted. The vessel began to shake quite hard.

"What's that rumbling about?" Captain hollered over the noise.

21

"We don't know, sir," said EXO hurriedly.

McKinley agreed, "Unknown, sir."

Officer Gwen offered, "Give me twenty-four hours, and I'll figure it out, sir."

Captain scoffed, "Twenty-four hours is something we don't have!" Then, insistently, "Where is our intel? Come on, hurry! It's good we're not guarding someone's back right now. They would be dead while we fumble around. We're better than that, so act like it!" He raised his voice and commanded, "Step on it! This could be our most dangerous and tragic mission yet, people, if we're not focused. None of us may go home alive. I don't want that to be you or me, Mr. Gwen! Understand?"

John, the brainiac and engineer, explained, "It's some sort of energy field, sir, coming directly from that object, now forty-two miles away."

"Energy field?" Captain repeated, scrunching his brow. "What sort of energy?"

John shook his head. "Maybe electricity, but out of this world and exceptionally strong."

Captain demanded, "How strong?"

"Very strong electrical energy, sir. But it also has EMP energy. It's confirmed. It has just neutralized certain ship functions," John said, a hint of anxiety in his voice.

"Which functions? It better not be communications, or engineering or our weapons. That is an act of war." Captain moved toward John to hover over his shoulder.

John swallowed. "Checking … still checking. It has targeted only our weapon systems, but all of them, including our top secret ones. This is a high form of intelligence, which is very well informed, and they are experienced warriors," John glanced nervously at Captain. "They were prepared to confront us in particular. But I don't know who they are or who trained them. They are ready for trouble with us. They saw us from more than forty miles out, before we noticed them. They fired on us from there, accurately, from 9,000 feet beneath the surface. They took all our weapon systems completely down. We are already engaged in war, and we never got to send an ambassador, nor request terms of peace, nor fire a warning shot, nor even see the enemy. So far, this war is all one-sided."

Captain hollered, "Battle stations!" Hurriedly the men scurried everywhere to their positions. Then, gulping for breath and fearing it may have targeted life support functions like oxygen, he asked, "Is it an armada of submarines? A division?"

"No, sir. It's only one object, not many."

Captain grasped, "Is it Russian? Chinese or Israeli?"

John tensed, shaking his head. "Definitely not, sir. Its abilities far exceed any of their capabilities or anything they've been testing."

Captain asked tersely, "Are you sure of this?"

John replied, "I am, sir. Nearly 100 percent sure." He was thinking to himself, *If we're at war, then why did this object let us live? We're already down; why not finish it and fully take us out? Do they want hostages? Prisoners? People to torture?*

"Wait!" John exclaimed, raising a hand to his headset. "There is a soft, low-pitched sound emanating from it. It's an energy frequency disruptor. Oh, perhaps our mystery vessel might be a yet-unknown creature, like an electric eel. It's stressing every joint on the boat. I theorize if it raised its voice to a high pitch, like an opera singer who breaks glass with the perfect high note, our whole sub would break into little pieces. There wouldn't be enough left of us to bury, fish to swim through at the bottom of the sea, or anything to be pulled up from our wreckage years later. If this is a creature, its pitch is perfect, its voice is powerful, and its sound easily carries across great distances. It can isolate one target at a time, like our sub, like our weapons, and leave all else intact. It can take us anytime it wants. It can defend itself effectively from afar." John's expression was a mix of fear and disbelief. He said quietly, "I suggest this information be kept secret from everybody."

Captain barked, "What? You've got to be kidding me!"

John held Captain's gaze. "No, sir. I'm afraid not, sir. This thing could electrocute our sub with deadly high voltage bolts. Do not provoke it, or it will fry us all."

"What's your advice?" Captain sighed, squeezing the bridge of his nose.

"Ask for terms of peace, sir," John said firmly. "The thing will be in clear visual range soon. Maybe it will want to talk, or better, listen. We still have our communications, engineering, and life support systems working. The creature left us with the ability to run. Perhaps it wants to chase us, sir.

Given that our weapons are down, it seems like we're being hunted. Can we call for help? But realistically, any help we could get would be ineffective."

Captain, thinking out loud, replied, "Hunted for what? Why would it do this to us?"

John, puzzled and shrugging his shoulders, now sighed. "Beats me. For glory? For food? Trouble is, it isn't possible. None of this is."

Captain nodded once. "We'll see. John, do your best to discover an effective counter to this thing, whatever it is out there. And get those weapons operational fast! I'll immediately contact Rear Admiral Smith for aid."

John nodded. "Aye, Captain. I'll do my very best."

Captain turned to leave, saying over his shoulder, "I agree absolutely about this being kept hush, hush. It would cause panic and despair."

"I'm sorry, Joe, but there is no help available that I could send you for something like this," Rear Admiral Smith grunted. "Don't trouble anybody else about this, either. That's an order. The Joint Chiefs are with me. They heard you, and this is their decision as well. Your country is obligating you and your crew alone to beat this thing. We can trust no one else to cope with and to counter such a threat." There was a beat of silence before he finished, saying, "You and your men are on your own. Good luck. Over and out."

Captain hollered, perturbed, "Good luck?" He shook his head to himself. "To think that I lived to see a Rear Admiral and top Chiefs fail to support their loyal captain and crew in an almost certain life and death emergency. That's like my own country feeding me and my men to the piranha! I didn't imagine I'd ever see that. Well now, we're in the thick of it, like it or not. Is this Normandy revisited, the March of the Light Brigade, or Gallipoli? I can't tell the crew, none of them, for it would break down morale and could cause mutiny. I need each of them at his very best to survive today."

He prayed privately in his mind. *God, I am going to need Your help on this one, or I'm in the sink and we'll all die. Quite possibly we could die very, very soon. Help, Lord! Save my men, and hurry. I can't believe that this is really happening. Why did I get out of bed this morning? I will to God that He would show us what the enemy is and what to do about it. This is all surreal, or even sinister. Does the USA now leave soldiers behind? Is our flag still standing and waving for freedom? Have we been conquered by a hostile country? Does our top brass have a gun to their head? God, why didn't You warn me in advance that all this would happen?*

"What in the world is that?" Chief asked, wide-eyed.

The Chief was trying to hide his trepidation at this moment, somewhat unsuccessfully, as he saw an immense creature on the sonar screen. Having arrived in the Indian

Ocean, the captain and the EXO opened the sealed orders, which only made matters worse for everyone. With all their weapons systems down, it also seemed like a very bad joke, both outrageous and hopeless. The orders said, "You are entering savage, unconquered territory, and you will be fighting a monster with unknown capabilities. No one else has been successful. No other submarine would we dare to task with this. We're giving you the great honor of destroying this monster. You have permission and authorization from the President of the United States to use all your nuclear weapons against this thing. Here are the missile launch codes. This creature has been 100 percent effective in killing every military adversary sent against it; every boat, plane, submarine, ship, and every group of submarines from various countries. They all attacked; they all sank; there were no survivors. The only transmission that survived was that it's black and formidable and gigantic. Your orders are to do whatever is needed to stop it from sinking our warships. Kill it, make friends with it, drug it, or do whatever is necessary to fulfill your mission."

The captain and the EXO stood breathless. They were thinking, "100 percent effective at leaving no survivors? This is insane! What a cruel mission. It's unreal."

"We're being made a sacrificial lamb. Food for a wild beast and a superior enemy. This isn't fair!" EXO panicked.

Captain's brave disposition quickly faded at the news. "This is a job for Saint Francis! They call it an 'honor.' I don't see that—a suicide mission more likely. What glory is there in that? We have wives and children back home. To die feeding the fish is not exactly the legacy that I want to leave to my descendants. None of us do. I am not afraid to die for my men or my country, but over this? If it was me, I'd leave it alone and tell all others to steer clear and head somewhere else, somewhere less threatening. God help us! However, we have orders—so let's do them with pride. It's our job. We gave our word to our God and country, so that settles it. Let's get to it!"

EXO, with pride rising in his voice, managed, "That's my Captain!" But he quickly dropped his head and looked very far away.

"I bet Saint Francis felt inadequate too," offered Chief Blackstone, "but the animals knew better; they admired him. He was a holy man and so are you. You're my mentor in holiness, and that of others. The officers and crew respect you, and so do I. I trust you. Remember the words of Robert Murray McCheyne, 'A holy man is an awesome weapon in the hands of God.' You risked your life for ours several times, and you didn't complain. I saw you. I'm behind you."

EXO chimed, "Me too!"

Captain softened his face. "You both are wonderful." Then the captain was silent, pondering aloud, "This is way over all our heads. How do I get any of us out alive, given our orders?"

"It was God, not man, who sent us to the Indian Ocean to triumph, to save lives," Chief determined. "The Joint Chiefs are God's chess pieces to move on His board, and so is this creature. You're the right man for the job, Captain, and God will work through you. This creature will meet his match in the next few days."

Captain nodded shortly. "Thanks, Chief."

John entered the room swiftly. "Still nothing, Captain. No strategy of defense. However, the creature is calm and showing no signs of aggression. Are we now going to run our fastest from this monster?"

Captain hesitated. "Maybe not. Let's pursue the creature to learn more about it since it has stopped shaking the boat. That's our strategy, and our only option left. Make peace and friendship with it. Make it so."

Captain ordered Sea-Scan to be launched to take pictures. The captain also made a wise addition in his boat's records. "Don't attack or try to hurt the creature or any sea creatures. It seems amenable to peace and friendship for the moment."

The Captain wrote down a very short prayer for them to recite together. They all prayed it in unison. "Lord, help us to be the best soldiers, to make the best decisions and not provoke this beast."

Captain advised, "Let's remember this. We may have to recite it again."

EXO nodded curtly. "Aye, Captain. To make peace with it, this will be a hard sell to the crew."

Captain sighed in resignation. "Let's inform the men gradually and slowly, section by section."

Torpedo man Willie Jones had read a book called *Godzilla, King of the Monsters.* "I don't think anything like that is likely, or even possible. Enormous monsters? Ha! Do you?" he said to the captain and John. There was a long eerie, awkward silence. They never replied.

Officer George Clark, the communications man, peered at the sonar screen. "What is it?"

Officer Jeffrey Brown, in a low voice, said, "A very unusual whale, heading our way pretty fast. But this is no ordinary whale. Its speed alone is unbelievable. He's a huge whale. A big goliath he is."

Captain, attempting lightness, asked, "If he is Goliath, then who is David?"

Officer Brown didn't return the tone. "I'm afraid that we are, sir."

There was an uneasy silence.

"Maybe it's something mechanical like on 'GI Joe,' an enemy sub or a bomb. Or a spy device merely disguised as a whale. Or something alien," chimed one seaman. Concerned, he added, "Do you think I'm nuts?"

Officer Brown shrugged. "Maybe this thing will prove us all to be nuts. Whales don't move that fast. Let me back-track—no, it's not mechanical. No, not bionic. No, not alien; I've already checked for that. It's definitely alive and not controlled by man or aliens. And it's definitely a whale, and he's fast."

He paused suddenly, a look of shock on his face. "Wait a minute, it just rolled completely over, like a spinning drill bit piercing the water, a 360-degree roll, and increased his speed by six knots—eight knots—more … wow! It's really racing toward us! Is it crazy? It's 3,000 yards, 2,500, 2,000 yards, 1,500 yards, 1,000 yards, 500 yards, and closing in. This guy's fearless, as well as fast. Let's torpedo it right out of the water. This couldn't be an ordinary whale; it's too fast; no way."

Just then, Sea-Scan, for a quick moment, got a distinct picture of its enormous black head, with white teeth gleaming. Officer Brown's heart skipped a beat. His mind drifted for a second, but he quickly snapped out of it and attentively watched and listened to the sonar sounds. The whale was still bearing down on their sub, like a colossus, coming into closer visual range now, and daunting. Suddenly, for no apparent reason, the whale slowed down almost to a halt.

Captain hurriedly asked, "From his sounds, Chui, what do you think he's saying?"

"Something like, 'Don't try anything stupid, USA *Detroit*, or you'll greatly regret it!'" said Chui.

Captain looked to Enoch. "What's your take?"

"He's no bluffer, sir," Enoch breathed. "He's the real deal, a genuine terminator."

"Running Bear," Captain barked. "What's your take?"

Running Bear said quickly, "Sir, he's warning us and scaring us this time around, but don't press him again, or it'll be total destruction."

"Full stop!" yelled Captain. They could hear the engines winding down. He and his EXO, looking at their watches and counting down from 20, 19, 18, 17, 16 …

Enoch, at 15 seconds, quickly asked, "Should we flood the tubes, open outer doors, and fire? We're running out of time fast."

Captain commanded over the loudspeaker, "Hard right rudder!"

Officer Fred, the pilot, nodded, "Aye, Captain."

The crew all gripped on to something strong to keep from falling.

Captain ordered, "Keep our head facing his head directly. We can't afford to be rammed from the side. We'll meet him head on; stay on his nose."

EXO grumbled, "That's the biggest nose I've ever seen or imagined."

A seaman shouted, "344 yards and still closing."

Captain commanded, "Everyone brace yourselves for impact. Hold on to something sturdy. This could be rough."

The crew gave a worried look, wondering why this might be so rough. They hadn't heard the sealed orders read yet. All grabbed something immoveable, but there was no impact.

"His body language and heart rate don't suggest an attack mode or fury," noted Officer Brown. "Maybe he's just playful or showing off, like he's having fun with us. Or maybe establishing dominance and territory."

"You mean, like a dog growling and showing his teeth?" asked a sailor.

Officer Brown raised an eyebrow. "Maybe. I hope that's all it is."

The sailor widened his eyes. "Well, he's sure got me shaking!"

"What does its voice sound like? It's tone? What does it suggest?" asked Officer George Clark.

Officer Brown gestured with his hands. "It's a very deep bass voice, a *clang-clang* sound, but it's kind. There's no rage in it, or malice or evil. It's a penetrating voice but peaceful, and very distinct and clear. I have a hunch, at least for now."

"I think he wants to communicate with us," said EXO.

Captain nodded. "That's good, let's not provoke it. How penetrating?"

EXO explained, "Ichthyologists tell us a whale's voice carries for thousands of miles with clear, distinct, and intelligible sounds from one continent to another."

The captain was encouraged a little that their foe was a whale, a creature he had liked and admired since he was a small boy. "I've always had a soft spot for whales. I pray he has one for us. How old is this thing?"

EXO thought for a moment. "It's hard to say, but given its superior size, probably very old and wise. Just think, we found it. He could be a direct descendant of Jonah's whale in the Bible. Jonah's whale was exceptional in many ways, off the scale even for a very big whale. Famous for size, power, and being peculiar. Having an exalted purpose and superior dread, intelligence, spirituality, and speed. Plus, he got involved in foreign missionary concerns."

Captain questioned, "You view him or her as superior?"

EXO looked sternly. "Don't short-sell him. He is quick, very smart, shrewd, and coordinated, and much older than all of us."

Seaman Roberts shouted, "Sea-Scan is back."

Captain turned to the pilot. "Make your dive; follow the coordinates; come left 120." He paused before asking, "How big is it?"

EXO whispered in his ear, then said, "Sir, you don't want to know—not now; not until we're safe and docked. I've muzzled Officer Brown on this subject."

"Why?" asked Captain.

"It could cause panic, sir, especially among the crew," said EXO carefully. "Let's just call its size *exceptional* for now. Panic is something the whale would detect, which would be unfortunate and could incite a sea fight. It could be unnecessarily provocative with high casualties. I suggest we don't tell his dimensions to the officers or to the crew. He's big, really big." He gestured with his arms and hands.

Captain sighed. "Agreed." The captain was looking troubled and feeling very old. "Exceptional is definitely the word. I've never seen anything so grandiose as I saw on the sonar. I can't get over this. A direct descendant of Jonah's whale?" He thought to himself, *What other whale in all history is this close in resemblance to Jonah's whale? Maybe God did bring us here for a great victory.*

Chief Blackstone interrupted, "I hate to break up this romantic fish story, but what's the likelihood of him ramming our submarine for real and injuring my sailors, or far worse? I have a lot of boys on board."

EXO calmed him. "Nil, if we don't attack it or hurt its family."

Captain nodded, his faith strong in EXO. "I concur with that."

Suddenly the whale veered to his right, and went diagonally underneath the submarine with a startling quickness. He began to circle it at such a fast speed that the submarine couldn't stay face-to-face with the creature, nor protect its sides. Although the beast did not slam them, he came so close that it made the submarine shake.

Captain let out a breath. "That was a witty move. Pilot, evade him. John, do you have anything for me?"

"No, sir," said John.

"Keep at it. He's potentially very dangerous, regardless of his purpose." The captain then thought, *I wonder what he is saying. What's his message? What's he after? Why is he acting so boldly? Is he onto something?*

Officer Brown noted, "He's slowing down now—a lot."

Captain dabbed at the sweat on his brow. *Whew!* he thought. *I hope he's exhausted himself and now needs to take a long nap. I hope he's just curious.*

At that moment the monster was tilting his head this way then that way as he got closer still, moving very slowly, studying the submarine, circling it, and probing it with his own sonar, listening with his keen ears, eyeing it, looking right through everyone and everything, sizing it up. His ears could even hear the voices and the heartbeats of the crew, assessing for strengths and weaknesses, sins and addictions. The crew could feel the whale probing them inside and out, and they struggled to keep it all together. Then the whale locked on to something in the Con room that justified every mile of his long and hot pursuit of the USS *Detroit*. The whale growled with certain hot anger.

As the whale moved to their rear, the captain took advantage of the opportunity, yelling, "All ahead full!" The command was echoed. The submarine took off, leaving the whale far behind. Officers standing on their feet tilted backwards. Those seated, their heads tilted back.

The submarine started moving through an underwater maze. Running Bear, the linguist, took the pilot seat as the captain spoke in English, moving at high speeds now. Then the captain started speaking in French. "Bonjour, c'est votre captaine qui vous parle . . ." Farther ahead, they traveled through another complex maze, speaking Spanish, German, and then Italian, trying to confuse the whale.

Captain ordered, "Now slow down to 30 knots."

The captain decided to find a deep place and make a sharp descent to classified depths, hoping to lose the monster. But Officer McKenzie said, "Captain, you won't believe this! He's staying side-by-side with us at this horrible dark depth, and he is relaxed and unstressed."

Captain chuckled, "I wish he'd teach me to be unstressed at a time like this."

Lieutenant McKinley warned, "The boat is definitely stressed at this depth. We'll have to break this off now."

Captain nodded once. "Do it, rise to 600 feet below the surface, pronto! Deep depths can't shake him."

"I think he's moving at us like a boxer," said EXO. "He keeps jabbing his right fist at us over and over and is keeping his left fist back for a knockout blow."

Captain raised an eyebrow. "What do you mean?"

"Our strategy of making friends may not be working," EXO grunted.

"No," Captain said with a sigh, "but we must stay on this approach and try to make friends."

In all five languages, the creature amazingly caught up and stayed on top. He accompanied the dive and was waiting for them when they came out of the maze of tunnels, deep caverns, and perilous ravines. He stayed beside them during the classified dive. The Captain had instructed the pilot to evade this monster. Nonetheless, the whale showed he was a brilliant hunter-tracker, formidable, and understood at least English, French, German, Italian, and Spanish, and was faster and more resilient than they thought.

The Captain, troubled, said to himself, *He's not letting us get away. He keeps up with us. He's even one giant step ahead of us, like a mind reader or a prophet, with a prophet's supernatural gifts. Why? To remind us of God's sovereignty, perhaps, and of how capable Jonah's whale was. How did he do it? So much for our success in running away from him, let alone waging war with no weapons. We must have something he wants. What? What* could we possibly have that he or she wants or needs? At any rate, we must not underestimate it from now on. Something tells me this is super serious to him. It's not a game; he's on a mission. And he's faster and smarter than I thought.

Then the whale started greatly decreasing his depth in the water, heading upward. With a burst of speed, like an arrow shot from a bow, a giant squid attacked him and tried to blindside the creature. The whale caught a glimpse of it and rammed it with his massive side before the squid tried to bite him. The whale then changed directions and ceased pursuing the submarine. Next he gave the squid a head butt, knocking him a considerable distance away. He followed this with a bite and a hold with his twelve-feet-long white teeth, while it was still stunned. The Black then took him down to a deep underwater boulder where he broke the squid's exo-skeleton and then swallowed him whole. As if nothing had happened, the whale went back to the submarine to pursue it.

The Captain ordered the pilot, "Go up to periscope depth and slow to 10 knots, and come right 45." Then he took a look outside. There was nothing interesting on the surface, with the very notable exception that this whale, too, surfaced at that very moment to catch a breath and take a look. Just as he surfaced, his snout released a higher blow than any whale on earth.

The captain thought, *Wow, it's so huge! It's the color black too. How ominous. Someone could have a heart attack just from seeing it rise up to the surface to pursue him or to greet him.*

What kind of monster, what kind of whale has such a huge, black, rectangular-shaped head?

The creature leaped out of the water completely, and yawned, showing its many big white teeth, its long mouth and its totally black body. And then, splash! The biggest splash imaginable, as he belly-slammed, while the Captain peered through the periscope.

Captain exclaimed, "You just missed the show, EXO! We've got clear visual sights of him up close. Unbelievable!" The submarine began to bob up and down under the whale's huge wake.

Chui cried, "Loco!"

Antonio, with big eyes and a dropped jaw, breathed, "Mama Mia!"

David, the beach boy, loudly said, "Hey dude, wicked!" The men looked at David like he was on something.

Another said, "Me Irish!"

Willie Jones said, "Like, he cool—and hazardous to our health. Later! I'm outta here!"

Captain asked, "Where are you going to go, Willie, in the middle of the Indian Ocean on a submarine?"

Willie grumbled, "Nowhere, sir."

The whale again started to growl.

Captain began shaking all over. "Whoa! Unfortunately, I think he understands our words, regardless of what language we're speaking. Be very careful what you say. He's listening to everything and understanding and reacting big time. Don't tease him! That means everybody! It could cost us our lives."

The crew responded, "Aye, Captain."

Enoch nodded. "No problem, sir."

Captain thought to himself, *He's got to be vulnerable somewhere, somehow. God help us to find it.*

Suddenly, there appeared a North Korean bomber coming against the beast, perhaps an instance of glory-seeking after hacking USA military transmissions. After a long, deep dive by the whale, near the ocean's muddy, dark, brown-gray bottom, the whale heard the noisy plane coming. As soon as they dropped their guided torpedo from the plane, the Black came up and leaped completely out of the water. It released its EMP energy. Then the torpedo sank like a rock. He cried with a high, blood-curdling note, melodious and with perfect pitch, and the plane instantly broke into little pieces, then burst into flames like fireworks. Its back-up warship and cargo freighter, both Red Chinese, also immediately sank. There were no survivors. The seamen on board the USS *Detroit* were left breathless.

Later that afternoon, the President of the United States' intelligence squad searched on the submarine's computer and found out its weapons were down. The President overruled the Joint Chiefs and the Rear Admiral, and sent an airborne torpedo plane with a full payload of guided torpedoes to drop into the ocean. The pilot's mission was to hunt down and destroy this foe that had dared to jam a leading submarine's total weapons systems, and had used the dreaded EMP weapon, considered as a weapon of mass destruction, violating United Nations rules of warfare. (The whale didn't get his orders from the United Nations!) The catch was that the pilot of this torpedo plane was Chief Blackstone's love of his life, his fiancée Captain Mary Braswell, a naval aviator. They had hoped to be married at the end of this submarine tour, and raise a family. Now her life was in very grave danger, unnatural danger, and all their dreams could die this afternoon, this very moment.

Mary sent a love greeting to the Chief. "Ed, my love! Do you love me, sweetheart?"

Ed managed to say, "Yes, I do, with all my heart! But ..." Ed was coming apart inside. How reckless was her intel to attack this dreaded creature? Why couldn't they leave her out of this? It was enough that Ed, Joe, McKinley, George, and company were sacrificing their lives for the cause. This was either a very bad sense of humor or horrible timing. *I wish that I was up there instead of her,* he prayed.

Then she issued a stern message: "USS *Detroit*, move at least five miles away immediately! Step on it! Stay clear of this thing. We're going to light up this ocean like a Christmas tree with explosives. We're about to blow it to kingdom come!"

The captain gave orders to dive and the submarine moved out of harm's way for the attack. The whale left off pursuing the submarine for a while. The Chief feverishly tried to warn and stop Mary's bombardier, and to get her to turn back immediately. Before he could do so, her plane threw everything they had at the Black. Torpedoes came fast from multiple patterns, speeds, and directions. But the whale heard them all hit the water and stopped, shook himself, and launched his EMP. Suddenly, all the torpedoes became like lead and sank to the ocean's bottom, out of power. The Chief grabbed the phone and shouted at the top of his voice, "No! No!" Then, "Mary! Mary, my love—are you alive? Are you alive?"

There was a long pause.

Then more silent waiting.

Tears began to fall.

Many minutes passed.

Still no response. Ed pounded the instrument panel with his fists, still crying, "No! No! No!"

Mary's voice finally sounded. "I'm fine, sorry we couldn't help you. I'm not hurt—not a scratch! Sorry for that big scare. But my gas is low, so I have to turn back now. We're on our way back now. I'm far away now. I'll miss you, sweetheart. Take care of yourself and your crew. Another bomber will follow ours to make sure the job is done correctly, today." The Chief was very thankful to God and, yes, to the whale, for tempering his anger and revenge, and his weapon, and not killing Mary as he did the North Koreans and Red Chinese.

The other bomber did come with the same result – the same merciful result. But they didn't kill or cripple the beast. The whale was unmoved.

The Chief couldn't wait to say prayers of thanks and go to sleep to release the overwhelming stress of the day's events. He passed out right away in bed.

A fourth group arrived in a privately-owned, high-flying military jet, representing the New World Order. They dropped a variety of biological weapons on the monster, and fired a weather weapon from Alaska. They killed millions of sea creatures and water birds but the Black was not beaten. And he was definitely going to avenge the millions killed. He fired back on the plane with his inner EMP, annihilating their plane and weapons instantly.

Why the difference? The Black killed the attackers in some cases and spared them in other cases, like Mary. Here was a possible key to befriending him. What could it be?

Not the difference in race?

Nor color?

Military smarts?

Not finances?

Not speed?

Not weaponry?

Not noise?

A definite "no" to all of these. After consideration and drawing contrasts of all groups, the captain, with the Holy Club officers, theorized that perhaps it's a friend to God's friends and an enemy to all His enemies. The two pilots who were spared were devout Christians and animal lovers. The North Korean and Chinese attackers were atheists and Communists who hated Christians and persecuted the church. They were also mean to animals. The New World Order was Satanist.

The crew was speechless. The whale's demonstration today was terrifying. They were all afraid that they would be next.

CHAPTER 3

STRANGE DREAMS

That night the whale refused to leave the vicinity of the submarine and did not sleep. Meanwhile the captain was troubled by scary dreams, and sensed an urgency to pray as if his life, and those of his crew, depended upon it. The resurrected Jesus of Nazareth was in one dream and a giant black whale was in another dream. Both dreams cited the Divine Commandment 'thou shalt not kill,' and said to "repent and judge yourselves, or else be destroyed. You have innocent blood on your hands. Cleanse it and remove it today, or perish." He woke up, wet with perspiration, trembling and very afraid.

Very early that morning, the captain shared his dreams with the Holy Club at Morning Prayer. "The message was, 'The King of the Sea says to turn from your sins and your evil path of life and to Christ immediately, or Hell will come down on you. You all have innocent blood on your hands.

Execute judgment or be utterly destroyed.' That's what my dream said. Perhaps this whale is a prophet?"

Officer McKinley shook his head in disbelief. "It's the strangest thing. Last night I dreamed a voice was saying, 'Thou shalt not kill,' and there was a broken stone copy of the Ten Commandments."

Chief Blackstone chimed in, saying, "I had a dream too! It said, 'Rachel is weeping for her children, for they were murdered.'"

EXO sat back. "This is weird, but I dreamed that God is grieved because we are protecting a pedophile and a murderer."

Officer George Clark nodded. "I woke up in a sweat too, for I heard 'Avenge my little ones or die the death.'"

Chaplain Gaines said, "I was approached early this morning by two seamen who had disturbing dreams last night of two little ones who were murdered, saying justice must be served or we will be destroyed." There was a moment of silent reflection in the room.

Captain finally concluded, "I'm leaning now to a more spiritual interpretation of the whale's mission. Given all this, I believe God is speaking these dreams to us, and this whale is God's messenger."

The Holy Club, in unison, said, "Aye, Captain."

Captain noted, "I believe I know who the murderer is. You do too."

The whale was humming gently now, as if he agreed.

The men were horrified. They had never had an experience quite like this before.

Captain ordered, "Allen, get on the radio and inform the base that we have suffered a malfunction by something out of our control. It may take longer than anyone thinks, but we are starting to make some progress in understanding the foe and meeting his terms."

Allen said, "Yes, sir."

George Clark commented, "No one at the base is going to believe this. We must hang tight and sink or sail together."

Officer McKinley breathed, "I think this whale wants our souls for God."

Captain went on the loudspeaker. "This is your captain with an urgent message. The officers and I have discovered that we have a murderer on board the submarine, and we have discerned that this whale has come to avenge the victims. We will do a ship-wide investigation to find the criminal. The whale will destroy us all unless justice is served. Chaplain Gaines will offer prayer aloud over the speaker because we have ethical and spiritual problems, and this is his department. Chaplain, the mic is yours."

Chaplain Gaines, over the loudspeaker, began, "Each one of you must decide for yourself what's most important in your life. Take the necessary time to reflect on that. If you believe in God and need to make peace with Him, do it now. If you know of any unjust killing, deal with it now before God. This is life or death, Heaven or Hell. It's as real as it gets.

"This prayer is not mandatory. But to those who desire it, feel free to pray with me. Let us pray. Heavenly Father, I have sinned grievously against You, too many times to count. Have mercy on my soul. I'm sorry for the grief that I've caused You and others. Forgive me all of my sins, for Jesus's sake. Wash me thoroughly from my guilt. I believe that Jesus died for my sins and rose again from the dead for sinners like myself. I desperately need You now. Grant me peace with You, righteous Father. Send Your Holy Spirit to help me obey Your commandments, and spare us all untimely deaths. In Jesus's name. Amen."

There were many who said "Amen!" They sounded like a choir, with voices of hearty approval and great relief from burdens carried too long.

The Chaplain offered the men private confession that he heard and gave counsel separately. Some men confessed to being party to an abortion, to elder abuse, substance abuse, or harming their families or themselves. Others confessed to neglecting children, cursing God or their parents, or encouraging others to try to kill those in authority. Others admitted to intentionally being cruel to animals. Some humbly acknowledged that they attempted suicide and they vowed never to go there again. After the period of confession and counsel, the chaplain followed up on each of the men with many other good words.

EXO, leaning toward the captain's left ear, whispered, "Captain Davis, we'll get in trouble for this. Joe, it could be serious."

Captain nodded. "I know, they'll call us nut cases and order us to see a shrink. But they charged us to stop the whale, and we're going to do it the best way we know how.

They're not here dealing with this very strange life-and-death situation."

"Agreed," said EXO, "and it's not like you are alone. There are too many of our men who had the same dream."

But some grumbled the whole time. A Jewish officer with red nose and lips quivering said, "The name of Jesus is not to be tolerated in this man's navy. The captain and that clergyman must be censored for this."

Another, an atheist, said, "He doesn't have the right to force his religion on us. When we get back to base, I'll see they are both defrocked."

Another, a Satanist, said, "They both ought to be executed for that kind of display. It's totally against the Constitution. The first amendment forbids it. They are traitors! This is not God's world, nor His creation, nor His country. They're going to hear about this!"

The captain ordered the pilot to slow to 15 knots and go up to periscope depth. Through the periscope the captain had a clear picture of the whale.

The ship's EXO was very knowledgeable about animals and whales, so Captain called him to the periscope to take a peek and to identify its kind. Just one glance and EXO said, "It's a bull sperm whale. He is the world's largest and most formidable predator. The word 'sperm' is just an unfortunate name that comes from having oil in his head, marketable oil. And spermaceti, a valuable, waxy material used to make salves and candles. His intestines often have ambergris in them, which is used for a very expensive perfume that creates a lot of money and power for whale poachers. It's definitely a male. Females are only thirty to forty feet long, but this guy is in a whole other category. And being black, he carries a greater fear. In the animal world, his color means, 'Attack me and I'll kill you!' Most other sperm whales are gray and sometimes blue, so this one is dominant in the sea—an alpha. In fact, he's a super alpha since he had a 100-foot-high blow. A normal sperm whale would have a spout of some twenty-five feet high out of the water. This one might be a loner or a bachelor or a married scout, since most bull sperm whales travel with females. He will take about ten minutes to catch his breath now." The EXO gazed, transfixed, imagining how short their lives might be. "Our strategy must be: Don't attack the whale."

Captain said roughly, "That's what I've been trying to say for the past forty-eight hours! EXO, where did you learn all that?"

EXO smiled. "My Dad was a fisherman out of San Diego. Remember? And I love to read."

By this time, both the submarine and the whale were nearly standing still, side-by-side, as the wake from the big whale's periodic tail-slapping caused the sub to rock back-and-forth and to bob up and down uneasily. The tail-slapping felt like corporeal discipline to the men on the submarine.

The crew whispered among themselves. "He's not fully satisfied with us yet. What more can we do?"

EXO commented, "Whale experts call sperm whale tail-slapping 'the hand of God coming down.'"

"Do they eat humans?" asked Captain.

EXO shook his head. "They don't attack us or our boats unprovoked. Officer Brown, has he made a clicking sound?"

Officer Brown gestured back with his head, "No."

"If a sperm whale gets overwhelmed in a big fight with too many opponents, he makes a clicking sound that can be picked up many miles away, and other bull sperms will speed to join the fight and help him," continued EXO.

Officer Brown turned pale. "Can you imagine trying to fight a whole group of these whales?"

"I say kill the thing before his family gets here," said Officer Gwen. "Make sushi out of it. It's too close to our vessel. I don't like it."

Officer Craig Mislou questioned, "What if it sinks our mini-sub when we launch it and kills our SEALs inside? That wouldn't take much. They are supposed to have a mission today at 0900. He could be a big obstacle to their success. I say, while we are still in control of the situation and of this whale, blow it to kingdom come while we can. Flood torpedo tubes one and two, plot a solution, open outer doors and prepare to fire. I would call for sounding the alarm and combat stations."

"Officer Craig, you'll make a fine captain someday," said Captain. "A bit impulsive and over-confident, though, and there are facts you don't know or you wouldn't say such things."

"Yes, Captain," Officer Craig, responded humbly.

Captain continued, "As to us being in control, that is arrogance. This whale is far smarter than we think. He is calling the shots now. Since he is a divine messenger, we should be humble. We need to see if he'll give us leave to go peacefully. I believe that he'll detain us until all his conditions are met, or until we are destroyed."

Officer Frank scoffed. "You sound like you've already surrendered to this monster. Forget pro-whale feelings; you've got to kill this whale. Whale-hugger or not, you can't justify surrender. You're the captain in the proud USA Navy, and we don't surrender to the enemy."

Officer Brown shouted, "The whale is growling now!"

Captain retorted, "That's because you've been talking about killing this thing. This whale discerns our speech and attitudes." On the loudspeaker, the captain ordered, "All hands, think of as many reasons as you can to like this whale and whales in general. That's an order! It could save our lives."

The crew sounded, "Aye, Captain!" The crew began talking loudly of why they liked whales.

"Officer Frank, you don't understand this whale's capabilities. He doesn't care about titles, the USA, or the Navy," said Captain.

Officer Frank responded, "But *I* do."

Captain said sternly, "Then get back to your duties."

Officer Frank dared not say anything more.

CHAPTER 4

INNOCENT BLOOD

Four Navy SEALs, Bob, Charley, Teddy and Fred, departed safely on time for their mission aboard the mini-submarine. They were supposed to intercept and destroy an enemy assassin team that had terminated a number of high-ranking military officials. Charley manned the submarine as a get-away car while Bob, Teddy and Fred executed a stealth operation on land. The SEALS' mission was effective, but during a firefight in an undisclosed location they got separated and had to flee. When Bob and Fred swam back to the submarine, Teddy was missing. The team exhausted their resources searching for Teddy, but they couldn't find him. They regretfully listed him as missing in action, and feared he may have been killed. Their hearts were heavy because Teddy was one of those special ones. He was their devotional chairman, the most apt to pray for them and to recite scripture. Teddy had often said, "Spies tend to be spiritual types, knowing that we could die on any mission and meet the Creator." Teddy's loss was too painful for them to be satisfied with their exploits. Bob, Fred and Charley reluctantly departed for the USS *Detroit*. Though they had carried out orders, they felt defeated.

"Officer Gwen, so you are afraid of our whale? Of it being so close?" asked Captain. "I am too, but for a more transcendent reason."

Officer Gwen spat, "There you are, forcing your religion on people again. That's what is wrong with this country. 'Believe in Jesus or go to Hell.' That's our worst problem. Our biggest threat to freedom and happiness. You think that the whale is on you Christians' side and against us pagans." By now, Officer Gwen was yelling loudly with red face and neck. "Wait till the base hears from me that you endangered this sub and crew for what you call a 'Christian whale.' They will relieve you of office, I promise you. You'll be court-marshalled. And another thing, that Bible of yours is so condemnatory. Talk about a guilt trip, it takes the cake. It's poisoned our lawmakers and law books, telling people that what you call 'rape, murder, adultery, and perversion' are evil, even criminal. Nothing is criminal, not even torture, drugs, or kidnapping. These happen all the time, even in the Navy. It's how we have our fun, and fun is never sin. Morality is a fiction, and so is religion! Darwin proved that. Face it, we're animals. And it's none of God's business. Our only principle is don't get caught. The 'Lord,' as you call Him, needs to keep His own law against judging. We're going to get our revenge on the Bible—and on whales by using them for target practice. We will send them to their deaths and cause another big whale shortage! A lot of gutted, beautiful, dead whale bodies strewn on the shore! Get yourself a good attorney, Captain!" By the end of this rant, Officer Gwen was laughing.

Captain countered, "You first. Officer Gwen. You are under arrest as a suspect in the double kidnap, rape, torture, and murder case of Angelo James Roberts, an eight-year-old boy, and his little sister, Emily Ann Roberts, who was six years old."

The captain told Chief Blackstone, "Bring two other seamen and bind Officer Gwen. Hold him in sickbay under armed guard. Search his belongings for evidence too. Quick!"

Chief said quickly, "Aye, Captain!"

Officer Gwen hollered, "I'm a martyr for the cause! A hero! You hear me? A hero! A hero! A hero . . ." His voice faded away as he was dragged off by the Chief and two other seamen, who were relieved at finally apprehending this criminal, widely-suspected by many on the submarine as a pedophile, a murderer and a torturer of animals.

Captain, exasperated with Gwen, scoffed, "A hero! Him? Whatever."

A few minutes later, a seaman returned with something that resembled a bowling ball. He said, looking scared, "I bowl, but this is no bowling ball. It's too heavy, and it has no place for your thumb. It gives me the creeps."

Captain ordered, "Keep it as evidence. EXO, you have the Con. Surface the sub and have a helicopter pick up Officer Gwen to deliver him for confinement and military court. And replace Officer Gwen's position on the Con."

EXO nodded. "Yes, sir."

The captain took the ball to sickbay to question Officer Gwen in the presence of two guards. "Everything is being recorded. You have the right to remain silent. What is this?"

Officer Gwen stated, "A crystal ball given to me by my grandmother."

"Why is it in an officer's possession, and why did you bring it aboard the sub?" questioned Captain.

"It's a way to see and talk with Satan," Officer Gwen smiled menacingly.

Captain pushed further. "Did Satan order you to kill Emily and Angelo Roberts?"

Officer Gwen's smile grew. "Exactly." He started laughing hellishly and couldn't stop. "And I'm going to get away with it!"

The captain thought to himself, *Give a fool enough rope and he'll hang himself.*

Captain responded, "I don't know when I've ever encountered such evil before in one person. No wonder the whale has such a problem with our boat. May I offer you the services of a chaplain before you are carried away?"

Officer Gwen scoffed, "No! You must be kidding."

CHAPTER 5

RESCUE OPERATION

The helicopter arrived to pick up Officer Gwen. He whispered seditiously to the guards as he was being escorted away. "The captain is crazy! He's gone completely nuts! He's going to get you all in a deep sea crisis where the sub is crippled. He will lose the sub and start a nuclear war. Mark my words! You'll be sympathizing with me before you know it."

One of the guards gave him a look and sharply rebuked him. "Shut up! The captain is right. You've finally been caught and shamed. You're absolutely disgusting, so zip it or I'll kill you myself."

He finally zipped his mouth shut, but he tried to start a physical fight by shoving the two guards with his shoulders before he was lifted into the helicopter.

Seaman Stephen, a man from Rhode Island, said with a strong East Coast accent, "There is a lot of stupid out there."

The whale kept the submarine in his sight until Officer Gwen was fully gone.

Captain commanded, "Submerge to periscope depth."

"Aye, Captain," said Pilot.

Suddenly the whale took a dive without explanation and came back 80 minutes later. Through the periscope the captain noticed the whale was approaching on the surface. Was this a peaceful approach or was the whale creating more aggression? As the whale stopped, the captain noticed he was balancing a human swimmer on his nose. Zooming in on the periscope, he recognized the wetsuit as that of a US Navy SEAL.

Captain exclaimed, "Divers! Divers! Man in the water! Surface the sub and prepare to rescue a Navy SEAL. He looks wounded."

Two divers quickly donned wetsuits. As they exited the submarine and stood topside, one called back to the captain. "Captain, I've never disobeyed an order, but sir, I've never swam out to a monster before."

The captain compassionately replied, "I have a hunch it will be okay."

Fearfully, the diver said, "Aye, Captain." The two divers jumped into the water and swam out to the whale. The whale allowed the SEAL to gently slide into the arms of the two rescuers. The monster remained perfectly still as they swam him back to the submarine. Once aboard, the crew immediately recognized him. It was Navy SEAL Teddy Douglas. He looked pale and half-conscious.

"Rush this man to sickbay," said Captain hurriedly.

In sickbay, Teddy was resuscitated and said to the corpsman, "The whale is my friend. Don't shoot it. It saved my life." He then went into shock. Upon examination the corpsman found that Teddy had a bullet wound in his right arm, but had managed to stay alive long enough to be rescued by the whale. The captain called for another helicopter to pick up Teddy and deliver him to the Port of Diego Garcia. He asked Teddy, "Where are the others?"

Teddy shook his head. "I don't know. We got separated under heavy gunfire."

The crew was engaged in questions about the whole rescue. Why did the whale care? Why did he differentiate between a squid for food, and a man for rescue? How did he know when to leave and when to return before the submarine submerged? How did he know the man was in trouble, and to bring him to the submarine for help? Or was he reciprocating for the arrest of Gwen, as an exchange, as a King would: one destined to death, another released to life? Where are the other SEALS? Are they alive or dead or in trouble?

Captain took over the submarine's loudspeaker. "This is your Captain. I'm coming to believe that our whale is a moral creature. It cares about right and wrong, compassion and justice, life and death. Even human life. He proved it by saving our Navy SEAL, Teddy Douglas, from drowning. Plus, he spared two pilots and their crew, including Mary, our Chief's own betrothed. He values people. On top of this, he greatly prefers God over Satan." There was loud clapping and cheers in the background.

"Congratulations, men!" the Captain continued. "We have achieved our mission. There will be no aggressive actions toward this creature anymore. We must show it that we mean it no harm, that we're friendly. Engage the propeller, 20 knots. Head toward Diego Garcia to give a shorter distance to the helicopter. The whale can likely hear us talking, and he's proven he is smart. Plus, we have a 60-million-dollar computer telling me that this whale is protected by International Law. I'll inform the Big Brass that it has earned safe passage. The President and Joint Chiefs didn't know it was a sperm whale because we didn't know. We were sent to contact it visually and charged to make peace with it if possible. Those were part of our sealed orders. We can't kill it. Have I made myself clear!"

Many replied, "Yes, sir!" and "Yes, Captain!"

Seaman Tom, who was known as Crazy Tom, was shaking violently. "Permission to go to sickbay, Chief, to get some medicine? If that creature returns, he's going to use his fire the next time. I'm warning you, this whale is a highly advanced monster, so walk softly. Wait till we meet his wife! Don't offend her if you know what's good for you. They are partial to their wives and their own children, or any children of their kind anywhere."

Chief said curtly, "Go quickly and then get back to the engine room and man your station!"

The captain thought to himself, *He is closer to the truth than he realizes.*

Festivity was the result among men and animals. The whale now swam as if he was truly happy, playful and satisfied, putting distance between himself and the submarine.

There was a discussion on board, as to how someone becomes a beast, like Gwen. Most wanted to kill him for how he kidnapped, tortured, and brutally murdered those two little children, which many of them knew. The crew was relieved that justice would now be served. The Chief said, "No wonder there is an eternal hell. No lesser punishment will do." Many agreed.

Captain announced, "This sperm whale is brilliant, with a profound sense of justice. For the Bible says if we harbor a murderer, a rapist, or a kidnapper, then our punishment is the same as his. We had to get rid of Gwen or be killed ourselves." The captain gave a sigh of great relief. "Likewise, it was necessary that our men had a time of repentance and confession before God."

Officer McKinley addressed the crew. "Our captain did the right thing. I was there when brother Roberts got the news about his two kids. They are the sweetest and most loving couple you could ever meet. Their biological son, Angelo, was black, and their adopted six-year-old, Emily, was white with blond hair and baby blue eyes. He cried so hard he nearly died with grief. His wife, Margie, had a nervous breakdown. Their wake and funeral was unbearable." McKinley shook his head as tears welled up in his eyes. "They're our friends. People we love. I'll do anything to get to the bottom of this. I want justice." The crew all showed their support for what he said.

"This is a pattern," Enoch acknowledged. "We shouldn't just stop with Gwen. This plague has to stop."

"I will let the whole crew know what the military court decides about Gwen," said Captain, his face hard with grief.

Shortly thereafter, the mini-submarine arrived back at the USS *Detroit*. Bill, Charley and Fred entered the submarine with heads downcast. Bill said to the captain, "Mission accomplished, but we fear we lost Teddy."

"Be encouraged!" Captain grinned. "Teddy is alive and with us. He wants to see you. Follow me."

Charley entered sickbay first. "Teddy! You escape artist! We are so glad to see you!" All his comrades gave him high-fives.

"We have a helicopter coming to take him to Diego Garcia. It should be here shortly," Captain informed them.

When the other SEALS were confident that Teddy would be in good hands, they said their goodbyes to him with assurances that they would pray for him. They boarded the mini-sub and departed from the USS *Detroit* for their next mission.

Fortunately for Teddy, the USNS Mercy was on the east side of the Indian Ocean, near Java. As soon as he arrived in Diego Garcia, they transferred him from the helicopter to a heli-jet to be life-flighted to the USNS Mercy, a fully-supplied floating Naval hospital with a helipad.

The whale continued to follow the submarine as if there was something more on its mind.

CHAPTER 6

KING TITAN

Across the world, in the Mediterranean Sea, another US submarine was having an ordinary day. As they leveled off at 700 feet, they began to shake violently. They sent out a communique that they witnessed on the drone an unidentified whale of monster size fitting the USS *Detroit's* description, but a gray female. The beast went nonchalantly almost straight down by their starboard side into the great blackness of the ocean where the strangest creatures live and submarines fear to go. Minutes later, she was seen by the drone again, as she detected an aggressive, man-eating shark and gave chase. Terrified, the shark tried to out-maneuver the whale, but she was too fast. She pursued the shark, snapped at it with her large teeth and caught it the third time. She shook it violently and swallowed it whole. The shark had caused a human swimmer to drown by seriously biting one of his legs. The whale got it with human blood still on its teeth.

Word got to the USS *Detroit* and they marveled. The captain commented, "This second whale does not know what trouble she caused in the world by showing herself, proving that the Black isn't the only one."

Captain Joe Davis was now processing all that had transpired with the Black. "The Black is good."

"Yes. What shall we name him?" asked EXO.

Captain smiled. "I've got it: Regis Titanus. Or in plain English, King Titan, or just Titan."

EXO nodded. Thinking for a moment about the name King Titan, he responded, "Sperm whales have been known to attack whaling boats and small ships and sinking them when pressed and killing those who harpoon them and who kill their families. They are fighters, but they fight for worthy causes. They eat big creatures who fight back. They love a good fight. Like the lions of Africa, they ram their hostile dinner into a big boulder until they're senseless and swallow their opponent whole. See the intelligence? He's a king of the sea, as a lion is a king of the plain, a champion of contests at sea."

The whale must have liked his new name. He stayed about 1,000 feet from the submarine, while Sea-Scan was out front observing him for two weeks, back and forth. The EXO was curious as to why the whale stayed with them. He observed that King Titan kept chasing baby fish. Not eating them but driving them closer to the submarine. He wasn't playing with them, either. He looked very serious, and made sad, grievous sounds, as though some great tragedy had occurred in his life. Anxious to solve the puzzle, the EXO spoke privately with the captain.

CHAPTER 7

DOUBLE RESCUE

God was encouraging the whale to pursue his own heart now while the crew studied his actions.

EXO noted, "They don't prey on small baby fish, but that's all he's interested in these days. As far as I can tell, he has fasted this whole week. He is carrying something very heavy."

"Well," said Captain, "we already know he's intelligent and that he can see through our hearts as a divine messenger. Maybe he will let us understand his heart also. I'll wager that we could have him tell us what's troubling him."

Eager to try his theory, the captain ordered the submarine to slow to 10 knots and to surface and wait to see if the whale would join them. Instead, he beat them to the surface. The captain and the EXO climbed up on the sail and called to King Titan. The whale proceeded to teach the humans how to understand his language. He tried to use simple, human-like body language to communicate with them, gestures that might be recognizable to sons of Adam in general. His head hanging and groaning was to express sorrow. He raised and lowered his head quickly to say "yes," and moved his head side-to-side slowly to say "no." The captain and EXO caught on surprisingly fast.

Captain was in disbelief. "This whole episode reminds me of the Biblical story of Balaam and his jackass. We're the dummies and the beast is the teacher!"

EXO grinned. "Amazing. Let's try it."

Captain asked, "Are you grieving?"

"Yes," the creature gestured.

"Is it over a loved one?"

He gestured, "Yes!"

"Is it your baby?"

King Titan again gestured, "Yes."

Captain softly asked, "Did he die?"

Titan slowly shook his head. "No."

The whale gently slapped his tail on the water, and the humans clapped their hands, trying to copy him. Now he proceeded to teach them, by gesturing with his whole body and his right flipper to follow him. They followed him for about six miles. He led them to a series of fishing boats and their nets. King Titan surfaced to yank on the fishing nets, jerking the boats at the same time and releasing many captive sea creatures, including dolphins and other whales. Some men fell off their boats. "Man overboard!" Others threw out life rafts to save them. Some fishermen fainted in fear at the sight of the whale. A science-minded fisherman said, "Impossible! Why didn't they teach us this in grad school?" Conspiracy theorists among them swore it was the end of the world. Some thought it was the beast out of the sea in the Book of Revelation. A pragmatist yelled at King Titan, "You're stealing our money; a whole day's worth!" They fired guns and harpoons at the whale, which to him felt like nothing more than mosquito bites. But he was a hero to the whales he released.

King Titan had no time for fame and applause. He had to rescue his own. Single-mindedly, he quickly departed while the submarine followed him speedily. The captain said to the pilot, "Stay with that whale!"

Eventually the submarine and the whale both surfaced, and the captain and EXO continued their communication with King Titan from the bridge.

Captain continued. "Your baby was caught in man's fishing net?"

A quick, strong "Yes!" Plus, he leaped out of the water, happy that they understood.

"Are you and your family direct descendants of the Bible's whale in the Book of Jonah?"

Titan quickly replied a definite "Yes!"

Captain gasped. "Wow! I knew it! Are there others too?"

The whale responded, "Yes."

EXO wondered, "No ship could stop his rescue attempt so why does he need us?" They put that as a query to King Titan.

The whale did the same gesture again. "Follow me." This time he led the submarine to a nearby island with a beach, and let out a horrible wail, while they watched through the periscope. Then he swam back to the submarine.

EXO's face lit up. "I've got it! Your baby is on land."

The whale nodded. "Yes."

Captain asked, "What direction? North? South? East?"

At the word "east," the whale gestured, "Yes."

The captain slowly named as many countries he could think of east of the Indian Ocean: "Indonesia, … Philippines, … Marshall Islands, … Mexico, …"

The whale kept waving his head for "no." This took a while.

Lastly, the captain said, "The United States—"

King Titan nodded his head up and down quickly, then leaped out of the water again at how well his students were doing.

"Is it a boy?" Captain asked.

The whale nodded. "Yes."

For some strange reason the captain also asked, "Is it a girl?"

The whale replied, "Yes!" It was both.

EXO whispered, "How rare."

Captain looked to EXO. "Where in the United States would you take a whale if you trapped it alive?"

They both said together, "Sea World!"

The whale leaped out of the water and roared like a lion! That was it. That's why he needed their aid, to get his babies out of Sea World.

The Captain descended to the Con and called John. Plus, he invited anyone else who might know of a big baby whale catch that was transported to San Diego's Sea World recently.

"It's been on the news," said John. "The debut is in four days. They're Sea World's first sperm whales. Also, female sperms seem to be protesting. I mean, scores of them have been regularly ramming fishing boats in anger off San Diego. No deaths have been reported, yet."

An Arab named Nabi, upon hearing the captain's announcement, arrived in the Con. Nabi was born in Lebanon and was now an American citizen. He spoke fluent Arabic, English, and French, and could read and write in all three. He said, "My family caught and owns those baby whales. They caught them in their nets. Their fishing boat is docked at San Diego harbor." The whale growled.

The captain, John and Nabi proceeded quickly up to the bridge to communicate with King Titan.

The captain asked, "Are your wives ramming fishing boats?"

The whale nodded. "Yes."

"And you told them not to kill anybody, but just attack the boats?" asked John.

"Yes."

"This whale has character," exclaimed John. "I might flatten San Diego if they were holding my baby hostage."

Nabi said, "Legally, they are not under the ownership of Sea World until this Thursday at 4 p.m. Until then, I, as my father's firstborn and their owner, can go and release them and take them back before the contract is fully binding and give them back to the Black."

Captain said to Nabi, "His name is King Titan."

Nabi nodded. "Very appropriate. Forgive me, King Titan."

Captain, clearly afraid, said quickly, "Nabi, we have no time to lose!"

They called Sea World and spoke to the whale curator. He was furious, complaining about how much money they would lose, and that they would lose face before the public. He vowed to fight unless Nabi came to Sea World personally with several items of documentation, and signed for the whales' release. They were in the Indian Ocean, how could they possibly get to Sea World in three days with Nabi, the submarine and King Titan, who wasn't going to be left behind alone, waiting in anxiety. It was impossible. The Captain immediately recognized another snag, orders. He was told to arrive in Singapore tomorrow by Rear Admiral Smith. Given his last communication with the Rear Admiral, the captain was hesitant to converse again. But it was necessary to tell him "mission accomplished," at least in making Titan their friend and their ally. Maybe that way they could get some time off to help Titan regain his children. It was worth a try.

"Rear Admiral," said Captain. "Sir, the aggressor you sent us to stop is a gigantic and unusually intelligent sperm whale, protected by international law. Permission requested to rescue his offspring, a son and a daughter?"

"Not possible! You expect me to believe this?" Rear Admiral scoffed.

Captain explained, "We made peace with him. He's our friend and ally now, and he rescued Navy SEAL Teddy Douglas from drowning. I know it sounds crazy, and it's a long story, but trust me on this one. We need to rescue his offspring now."

Rear Admiral was shocked. "Why didn't you tell me? We'll discuss what happened later when you have more time. But for now, you may go save his son and his daughter. But I can only give you three days, no more. I'll get someone else to go to Singapore. By the way, the Joint Chiefs and the president are here with me. The president wants to speak to you, Joe, personally."

The president came on the line. "Fine work! Carry on, Captain. You've got my support. How can I help?"

Captain cleared his throat. "Mr. President, sir, what an honor to finally meet you. As to your question, I'm not sure yet. May I get back to you on that?"

"Sure thing. Over and out," said the president.

Captain was beaming. "Wow! The president asked to speak with me. But the trip is too far and too complicated, with too many snags. It's impossible."

King Titan gestured with his whole body and right flipper, indicating, "Follow me," at once heading for Red China. What was there?

CHAPTER 8

DEEP MYSTERIES

Driven by strong love for his children, the whale quickly accessed an underwater jet stream that literally carried him and the submarine at a constant speed and arrived on the border of Chinese territorial waters where they uncovered a volcano mouth a half-mile wide. They descended slowly. King Titan no longer seemed pressured for time. He knew something the rest didn't.

The captain had a hunch that something was about to happen, so he told everyone to securely brace themselves. This word was none too soon, for the whale, the submarine and a number of other unusual creatures were all carried by a highly advanced energy field through a tunnel. The entrance to the tunnel said in Arabic, "The Tunnel that the Nephilim [meaning, 'The fallen ones'], built. If you're not Nephilim, stay out or be destroyed!"

King Titan ignored their Nephilim threat completely. About forty Nephilim, visibly terrified of him, gave him room in the half-mile wide, perfectly-rounded tunnel. These half-devil and half-human hybrids, the remnant of a giant race from the time of Noah, built marvelous tunnels from continent to continent to quickly move worldwide, seize resources, capture human women, and dominate countries. They were a superior civilization, but extremely wicked and past redemption. The Nephilim fled deep within the earth to survive the ancient flood, and created a protective force field under the sea.

Officer Brown was glued to the sonar, radar and listening devices. They revealed forty giant human-shaped creatures moving in the tunnel alongside them, with King Titan. Officer Brown raised his voice in the Con so everyone could hear him. "There are giant people out there. Some of them are eighteen feet tall!"

"Cusco in Peru has unexplainable tunnels also, called Chinkana, which at least span hundreds of miles," John explained. "Archeologists have found giant skeletons of such creatures. The Bible mentions them also. Their goal was to obtain, marry, and impregnate as many beautiful human women as they could. They had insatiable greed borne of hatred for God and mankind. Noah's highly advanced world was largely destroyed behind their wickedness. These giants had six fingers on each hand and six toes on each foot, and their heads were huge and elongated with four rows of sharp teeth in their mouths. They ate people, wore no cloths, and were highly intelligent scientifically, especially in engineering designs and genetic manipulation. The Nephilim took control of many ancient countries, but it never occurred to me that I would actually see a living Nephilim." John's eyes were full of wonder as he said, "They must have survived underground."

"Horrible!" said Chui, pale in the face.

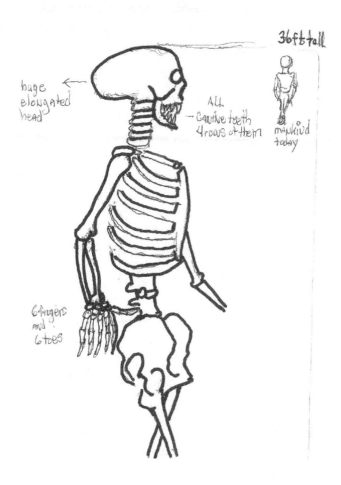

Some of the Nephilim tried to attack the submarine as it traversed the tunnel, but King Titan defended it by snapping seven of them in half, leaving only 33 alive in the tunnel. Their leader, Aristovartus, spoke in the language of the Nephilim, "Until next time, Black!" It was followed by a string of obscenities, insults, racist slurs, and forbidden profanity against him.

The whale replied in his own language. "I can't wait for a real fight with you, Nephilim! And next time, Aristovartus, join the fight. It is not fitting that all your men should die without their leader. That is, if you have the stomach to face me in my rage!" After that, they dared not to meddle with the USS *Detroit* anymore.

The energy field kept everyone safe as they traveled 11,000 miles in just a few minutes. It gently re-introduced the submarine and King Titan back to the ocean waters, exiting the tunnel through an inactive volcano on the ocean's bottom near San Diego. The submarine gradually decreased speed as they approached San Diego.

Before docking, Captain Davis made a call to the President, asking for a helicopter to carry Nabi and himself to Sea World immediately. He promptly supplied them with first class service. They docked in San Diego at 12:50 p.m. on Thursday, and then arrived at Sea World at 3:20 p.m. Nabi was rushed to the whale curator, who grudgingly released the two whales. The babies were guided to a channel underneath Sea World that led to the mouth of a bay, where King Titan and their mommies were anxiously awaiting their return in the open ocean. It was a festive occasion as they were released. The baby whales, all 4,000 pounds of each, were overjoyed to see their family, and did rolls, jumps, and tail slaps, and bounced off each other and their moms and their dad!

King Titan's harem of whales happily celebrated, and ceased ramming fishing boats. From there, Titan escorted all of them to another subterranean tunnel, taking them back to Australia. The President, the Joint Chiefs, Admiral Smith, and others had many questions about all this, but they decided to make this knowledge highly classified and to bury it in the Office of Naval Intelligence. Otherwise, glory-seekers would take photos of the monster, and create swarms of sleuths.

CHAPTER 9

ENEMY ATTACK

Following King Titan and his family through more subterranean tunnels, the USS *Detroit* was back in the Indian Ocean in less than five days. They were greeted by a wide variety of fish swimming near the submarine, including large-mouth bass and blue marlin.

Having successfully completed their first impossible mission, the USS *Detroit* was given a second dangerous assignment: to patrol allied waters around India, Australia and Java. The Rear Admiral and the Joint Chiefs had an uneasiness that something sinister was about to happen there. The USA needed sufficient fire power there to assist our allied bases. The *Detroit* rushed to offer police support.

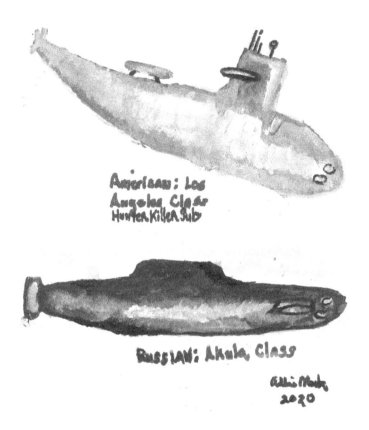

American: Los
Angeles Class
Hunter Killer Sub

Russian: Akula Class

Willie Martz
2020

Suddenly an unarmed torpedo sped over the submarine's top hull. Officer Brown at the sonar station announced, "The sound is of a fast North Korean submarine, resembling the Russian Akula class but fifteen feet longer and nuclear-powered."

"Battle stations!" Captain commanded, and the submariners dashed to their stations.

"Officer Brown," said Captain, "make an entry that the North Koreans have built a nuclear-powered submarine and have launched an attack against the USS *Detroit*."

The enemy submarine launched a second torpedo. This time it was armed, guided and deadly, and it was closing in fast: 1,000 yards, 700 yards, 500 yards, 400 yards . . .

A seaman shouted, "Torpedo has acquired and is homing!"

Captain shouted, "Launch countermeasures, a full spread!"

"Another torpedo is in the waters. Thirty-five seconds to impact, moving fast," said the seaman anxiously.

Captain shouted, "Sound collision alarm. Left full rudder. Reverse engines!" All three torpedoes missed the USS *Detroit*, and went off to seek countermeasure targets.

As the torpedoes were following maskers, jammers and decoys, the captain commanded, "All ahead full. Evasive action. Move right 45 fast. Step on it!"

The North Korean submarine quickly loaded two more torpedoes, readying to fire them. Simultaneously, they opened their missile silos and gave an order to launch a nuclear missile on Sydney, Australia, as the countdown was being given: 10, 9, 8, 7, 6, 5 . . .

Captain announced, "Launch cruise missile to intercept their nuclear missile as soon as it leaves the silo."

"Launch counter measures for torpedoes four and five. Fire torpedoes at North Korean submarine," said EXO.

While the USS *Detroit* was hurriedly executing its missile and torpedo launch procedures and opening outer doors, the *Detroit's* torpedo launch malfunctioned. All weapons were jammed. The officers remembered with horror that King Titan had immobilized their weapons!

Without warning, King Titan came straight up from the dark depths, full speed. With a deep growl, he hit the enemy submarine from underneath with his hard head and cracked it in half, dismantling it into little pieces and sinking it forever. The moment King Titan restored the USS *Detroit's* weapons systems, the captain ordered, "Fire on that nuclear missile! Knock it out of the sky. Fire anti-torpedoes." All counter attacks were successful. King Titan had acted in the nick of time!

Officer George Clark let out a breath. "Did we just start or end World War III?"

"Neither," said Captain. "King Titan just ended one that could have easily gone nuclear and possibly worldwide. He trusted us. He reinstated all our weapon systems, even the nuclear ones."

The whale whizzed by them for one last check to make sure God was fully satisfied with the crew.

Then he quietly swam away, leading his whole family like a trail of little ducklings, to patrol the oceans of the world.

"When did North Korea obtain technology for a nuclear submarine?" Chief questioned.

One sailor explained, "We found in Gwen's diary that he was collaborating with our North Korean enemies to destroy us on this very day, and he had a plan to escape had he not been arrested. He supplied them with our technology for a nuclear submarine. He really was a Benedict Arnold. A spy."

CHAPTER 10

COMING HOME

"**Goodbye, Mr. Titan,** king of the sea!" said Captain. "Take care. Thanks for everything. Words cannot express the world's, and our, debt to you, dear friend."

"That whale spared our lives over and over," Captain sighed. "He did wonders, and we still don't know what he's capable of. One thing is for sure—without him, this captain, this sub, and all of us would have been history. Now we must do one more patrol of the Indian Ocean. All ahead full. Set your angle at six degrees down. Make our depth 600 feet. Thereafter, maintain a speed of 26 knots."

"Aye, Captain!" hollered the officers.

After the skirmish came quiet. The USS *Detroit* did a circuit of Indian Ocean allied waters. There was no further enemy action. The Rear Admiral released the USS *Detroit*, having no further need for their services in that area. He congratulated them and concluded their emergency tours of duty.

The journey back took two weeks, as they were content to travel the conventional way. Word got out of their arrival in

San Diego. Outside on the dock, a crowd of anxious family and friends awaited their docking and exiting. There was shouting, leaping and tears of joy at their safe return. "Huh Rah! Huh Rah!" The weight of worry rolled off those who met them. The last ones to leave the submarine were Chief Ed Blackstone, EXO Craig Stevens, and Captain Joe Davis. They felt like they had received a great gift. They were humble, yet their body language exhibited a rare satisfaction.

Several disgruntled seamen of the USS *Detroit* did not forget their threat but carried it out. Captain Davis and Chaplain Gaines, with the whole Holy Club, were summoned before a tribunal and disciplined for Christian evangelizing. They were reduced in rank and ordered not to speak of Jesus Christ in the workplace again. Later, a higher-ranking officer overturned the decision and promoted them with higher honors. The officers got raises, perks, promotions and decorations. Captain Davis eventually became Admiral Davis, serving over the Admiral that disciplined him, and he became his boss.

Justice was served for the family of Emily and Angelo Roberts. Officer Gwen became the prime suspect in their double murder, and was tried and convicted by a military court. He was further convicted for trying to provoke the submarine to break international law concerning whales, for acts of racial hatred, for conspiring with the North Koreans by furnishing top secret information to them, and for his complicity in the attacks against the USS *Detroit* and against Sydney, Australia. Gwen was executed.

The EXO, Craig Stevens saw all his children grow up and married well. Ed retired and became a basketball coach for a Christian high school. Mary stopped flying and became a home-schooling, stay-at-home, country mom of five healthy children. Brenda joined the Holy Club. She and Jeff were happily married and they had two beautiful children. Until they were all old and gray, the crew of the USS *Detroit* told the story of King Titan to their children and grandchildren.

King Titan made peace with all those who upheld Christian character.

The End

APPENDIX

TRUTH IS STRANGER THAN FICTION

God has given the microphone to animals to speak to our lives quite a bit throughout history. Let's explore this in the Bible, beginning with Jonah's whale.

The Book of Jonah, Chapters 1 and 2

"**1:1** Now the word of the Lord came unto Jonah the son of Amittai, saying,

² Arise, go to Nineveh, that great city, and cry against it; for their wickedness is come up before me.

³ But Jonah rose up to flee unto Tarshish from the presence of the Lord, and went down to Joppa; and he found a ship going to Tarshish: so he paid the fare thereof, and went down into it, to go with them unto Tarshish from the presence of the Lord.

⁴ But the Lord sent out a great wind into the sea, and there was a mighty tempest in the sea, so that the ship was like to be broken.

⁵ Then the mariners were afraid, and cried every man unto his god, and cast forth the wares that were in the ship into the sea, to lighten it of them. But Jonah was gone down into the sides of the ship; and he lay, and was fast asleep.

⁶ So the shipmaster came to him, and said unto him, What meanest thou, O sleeper? arise, call upon thy God, if so be that God will think upon us, that we perish not.

⁷ And they said every one to his fellow, Come, and let us cast lots, that we may know for whose cause this evil is upon us. So they cast lots, and the lot fell upon Jonah.

⁸ Then said they unto him, Tell us, we pray thee, for whose cause this evil is upon us; What is thine occupation? and whence comest thou? what is thy country? and of what people art thou?

⁹ And he said unto them, I am an Hebrew; and I fear the Lord, the God of heaven, which hath made the sea and the dry land.

[10] Then were the men exceedingly afraid, and said unto him. Why hast thou done this? For the men knew that he fled from the presence of the Lord, because he had told them.

[11] Then said they unto him, What shall we do unto thee, that the sea may be calm unto us? for the sea wrought, and was tempestuous.

[12] And he said unto them, Take me up, and cast me forth into the sea; so shall the sea be calm unto you: for I know that for my sake this great tempest is upon you.

[13] Nevertheless the men rowed hard to bring it to the land; but they could not: for the sea wrought, and was tempestuous against them.

[14] Wherefore they cried unto the Lord, and said, We beseech thee, O Lord, we beseech thee, let us not perish for this man's life, and lay not upon us innocent blood: for thou, O Lord, hast done as it pleased thee.

[15] So they took up Jonah, and cast him forth into the sea: and the sea ceased from her raging.

¹⁶ Then the men feared the Lord exceedingly, and offered a sacrifice unto the Lord, and made vows.

¹⁷ Now the Lord had prepared a great fish to swallow up Jonah. And Jonah was in the belly of the fish three days and three nights.

2:1 Then Jonah prayed unto the Lord his God out of the fish's belly,

² And said, I cried by reason of mine affliction unto the Lord, and he heard me; out of the belly of hell cried I, and thou heardest my voice.

³ For thou hadst cast me into the deep, in the midst of the seas; and the floods compassed me about: all thy billows and thy waves passed over me.

⁴ Then I said, I am cast out of thy sight; yet I will look again toward thy holy temple.

⁵ The waters compassed me about, even to the soul: the depth closed me round about, the weeds were wrapped about my head.

⁶ I went down to the bottoms of the mountains; the earth with her bars was about me for ever:

yet hast thou brought up my life from corruption, O Lord my God.

[7] When my soul fainted within me I remembered the Lord: and my prayer came in unto thee, into thine holy temple.

[8] They that observe lying vanities forsake their own mercy.

[9] But I will sacrifice unto thee with the voice of thanksgiving; I will pay that that I have vowed. Salvation is of the Lord.

[10] And the Lord spake unto the fish, and it vomited out Jonah upon the dry land."

Did Jonah do something to provoke the whale in this account? At first glance the answer would be "No." But with more careful scrutiny it would be a resounding "Yes." One interpretation is that Jonah's bad behavior caused the storm on the sea. He also offended God. Jonah disturbed the whale's backyard, the sea. Plus, he offended his friend, God. To offend God was to offend the whale. Such is the mindset of animals.

But could Jonah's whale track his voice, his appearance, his very scent, and find him in a ship on the sea, or as a man thrown overboard? The sense of fish, such as sharks, to smell blood is well known. Salmon are distinguished in tracing back hundreds of miles to the very gravel and pond water where they were first hatched. How much more will the fish or mammal with the largest brain on earth have a tracking ability? The Lord recruited this great fish and inspired him with the knowledge to find Jonah, and to swallow this Hebrew prophet who had offended God.

Why would this whale care to obey Jonah's God? Or why would he give a little man a second chance on life, health, and ministry? Or why would he support God's mission and fulfill prophecy? Yet Jonah's whale did all these things because he had a spirit; a God-sense. This God was too strong for him to resist.

Sixty years before Jonah, in 700 BC, Isaiah the prophet prophesied that Assyria would turn to God and become His people. (Isaiah 19:25) The Assyrians were pagans. Therefore, Nineveh, Assyria's capital city and the residence of her king, had to be evangelized first to facilitate their conversion. In those days of Assyria, the King and his nobles had to be won over first. They needed an evangelist. God chose Jonah. Opportunities like this come and go quickly, so Jonah couldn't be late. The whale had a critical role in that. Jonah's whale signified a converted Nineveh, the Great City.

When Jonah hit the water and the whale swallowed him, a great peace and calm came over the sea. The storm ceased. The sailors were safe. God was satisfied.

Other animals come into the Biblical accounts where they play significant roles. Here are more examples from Scripture of how animals foreshadowed and signaled, even shaped, events.

In Genesis 8, Noah sent forth a raven and a dove from the Ark to test the level of the flood waters. These birds had the intelligence to cooperate with Noah's purpose, and they have since signified a whole new world after the flood. The dove brought back proof to Noah that the earth had emerged from the floodwaters (verses 7-12). Awaiting this day on the Ark were pairs of all kinds of land animals who, one year earlier, had found their way into Noah's Ark by some secret inspiration from Heaven (see Genesis 6 to 8). They ate the food which Noah had prepared for them, and they rested while on the Ark. When the floodwaters subsided, they went forth to find their ideal habitat and repopulate the earth. Amazing!

In Genesis 22:11-14, a ram, caught in a thicket by its horns, was a sign to Abraham that he didn't have to do a literal bloody sacrifice of his son Isaac on God's altar. It was providential that the ram was caught in the thicket at that moment. God provided the ram as a substitute. It was a foreshadowing of Jesus Christ, the ram of the covenant.

In Exodus 4, as part of Moses' training, God commanded that he grab a snake by the tail, and it became a staff in his hand. Moses gained faith and courage to face the most powerful monarch in the world, the Pharaoh of Egypt.

In Numbers 21, the Israelites were bitten by deadly snakes as a judgment upon their murmuring. God, however, provided a remedy. A brass serpent, lifted up on a pole, was a symbol of God's word, of Jesus Christ Himself, eternal life, and efficacious divine healing. When the Israelites gazed at this serpent, they were healed of their deadly snake bites.

In 1 Samuel 6, two milk cows, by their return of the stolen Ark of God to Bethshemesh, confirmed that it was God who brought destruction on the Philistines. The cows themselves greatly desired to resist the divine errand. They had never been yoked and they missed their calves greatly. They were full of milk and uncomfortable. But it was useless. They could not overcome the sovereign calling and power of God. "They went along the highway, lowing as they went, and turned not aside to the right hand or to the left." (6:12) After this toilsome journey, the cows became burnt sacrifices for Israel. Besides their role in returning the Ark of God, these two poor milk cows were another foreshadowing of Jesus Christ and His sacrifice on the Cross.

In 1 Samuel 10:2-11, the finding of the lost asses was a sign of the turning point in Saul's life. The Holy Spirit fell on him that day and he became a prophet, and subsequently king over Israel. Many signs were given in this episode, and two of them involved animals that were destined by God to be part of the prophecy.

In 1 Kings 17:1-6, ravens gathered food for Elijah at the command of God. Their natural tendency would have been to feed this food to their own kind. But God gave them a special mission to feed the prophet while he was hiding for his life.

In Matthew 21:1-11, the ass Jesus rode into Jerusalem signified the greatest revival in history through the death, burial, resurrection, and ascension of Jesus Christ. These events ushered in Pentecost, the Roman Peace, and the Christian Church. The ass and her colt were obedient servants of the Lord and pictures of what we should be as people.

In Luke 22:34, 54-62, the rooster that crowed in the Gospel was the signal of Peter's denial of Christ three times. The timing of the rooster's vocalization was coordinated by God Himself, and prophesied by His Son. The rooster's crow brought Peter to tears of contrition.

After Jesus rose from the dead, St. John 21 records a miraculous catch of fish, numbering 153, after a whole night of catching nothing. These many fish, by obeying Jesus' word, sacrificed their lives at His command to feed men.

Besides animals being appointed to foreshadow and shape events, they can be avengers and enforcers of God's law. God communicates with animals to carry out specific and limited judgments. Here are some examples from Scripture.

Exodus 7-12. The plagues of Egypt included myriads of reptiles, amphibians and insects bringing judgment on Egypt for her sins against God. These creatures knew their boundaries and only plagued the Egyptians, not the Hebrews in

Goshen. They were also assigned to attack Egypt's gods and to humiliate them.

In 1 Samuel 6:4-5, mice plagued the Philistines for stealing God's Ark of the Covenant. The Philistines were glad to send the Ark back to God in Israel.

During the times of the Kings, lions were particularly used by God as avengers. In 1 Kings 13, a lion slew, then guarded, the dead body of a man of God. The man had doubted and disobeyed God's express command. The man of God's ass also guarded the dead body. The lion did not eat the man's body, but protected it. The lion also defied his nature by not eating the ass. In 1 Kings 20:35-36, another man heard the word of the Lord and disobeyed it. A lion also slew this man for his noncompliance. In 2 Kings 17:24-28, lions ate multiple Samaritans for failing to fear the God of Israel and to properly worship Him. The king of Assyria then selected a true priest to teach the Samaritans how to fear the Lord.

In 2 Kings 9:36, wild dogs ate the wicked Queen Jezebel who promoted Baal and Astoreth worship, rather than worship of God in Israel. Elijah had prophesied Queen Jezebel's death for her many whoredoms and murders, and he was specific that dogs would eat her. The dogs carried out that word years later, just as prophesied. Who told these random dogs to eat Jezebel? A dog can be an avenger, and a dog can hear God.

In 2 Kings 2, forty-two children were slain by two she-bears for blaspheming God's prophet, Elisha. Animals realize that the true God is to be greatly feared.

As men often don't heed their prophets, priests or parents, so God occasionally speaks to us good counsel through animal behavior. In one striking case, God opened the mouth of a jackass and gave her intelligible speech. The Book of Job has numerous descriptions of a variety of creatures instructing us about ethics.

In Numbers 22:21-33, The prophet Balaam's life was saved by his jackass. It is noteworthy that while Balaam was spiritually blind, his jackass saw an angel of the Lord and perceived his purpose before Balaam did. But Balaam was hard-headed and he was not paying attention to God. Balaam abused his jackass but she defended him.

The animals in Job are examples of the Creator's handiwork, and they teach us virtue. In Job 24:5-6, the wild ass always has enough to eat as he rises early to work. In Job 39, God uses numerous wild creatures to repeatedly teach us humility. The ostrich teaches people that wisdom and understanding come from God. The Lord gives the horse courage to run into battle. In Job 40:15-24, God gives "behemoth" ten verses to teach us that our maker provides for us. "Leviathan," in Job 40, is a preeminent example of a creature to make us swallow our pride.

Holy Scripture also highlights animals as examples of wisdom, hard work, righteousness and trust. A study of animals in the Bible can show men and women how to live successfully. Job 12:7-10 tells us to learn from the wild beasts:

⁷ But ask now the beasts, and they shall teach thee; and the fowls of the air, and they shall tell thee:

⁸ Or speak to the earth, and it shall teach thee: and the fishes of the sea shall declare unto thee.

⁹ Who knoweth not in all these that the hand of the Lord hath wrought this?

¹⁰ In whose hand is the soul of every living thing, and the breath of all mankind.

Consider these additional passages.

In Proverbs 30:25, God even uses little ants to teach us. Ants are organized, and they plan ahead. The chapter also highlights the virtues of conies, locusts, spiders, lions, and the greyhound.

In Matthew 6:26, birds teach us not to worry. Worry shortens one's life and reduces its quality. Birds trust God for what they need.

In Matthew 17:25-27, a small fish with a coin in his mouth was how Jesus chose to pay his taxes, and Peter's, too. The fish illustrates obedient trust in God. It only did what it was told to hold a coin in its mouth until it was caught. That act made it famous! Through the example of this fish, Jesus showed his trust in the providence and provision of God, even over finances.

People and animals don't live in a void. Let's look briefly at the larger context of our world. Creatures are surrounded by winds, rocks, soils, vegetation and many other natural features that were fashioned by the same Creator and serve Him in ways He directs. According to Holy Scripture, these have a voice and a position in God's order. When Jesus rode into Jerusalem and children loudly praised him as the Messiah, Jesus said if the children had not cried out, even the rocks themselves would have done so. God made all things, great and small, animate and inanimate, to glorify Him.

In Genesis 6:13-7:12, the great flood showed that the inanimate creation will not bear with wicked creatures; it will destroy them. The waters were given a mission of judgment and cleansing by God. Only those persons and animals whom God chose survived.

In other cases, waters were a miraculous provision for people, animals and plants. During their wanderings in the wilderness, the children of Israel drank from water that came out of a rock. See Exodus 17:3-7 and Numbers 20:7-11. In I Kings 18:2, 41-45, Elijah called down rain from heaven. The rain harkened to the voice of Elijah because of the power of God in his life. Elijah's prayer ended a severe three-and-a-half-year drought and famine in Israel.

Natural features such as the sun, moon and stars were designed by the Creator as signs (Genesis 1:14). These signs indicate special times and seasons such as summer and winter. The Star of Bethlehem eventually foretold the birth of the Messiah. A rainbow after the flood was a sign of peace between God and man (Genesis 9:12-17).

Trees became a deadly opponent to Absalom's army: "the wood devoured more people that day than the sword devoured. (2 Samuel 18:8) Soundwaves served God in David's time. A loud marching sound in the tops of the mulberry trees was David's sign to go to battle, where he decisively defeated the Philistines. (1 Chronicles 14:14-16.) In Exodus 9, the plagues of Egypt not only included creatures, but darkness, blood, hail, thunder, fire, and a deadly mist.

According to Romans 8:22, the whole creation groans and longs for the day of resurrection and Christ's return, and our glorification with Him. It is written in the fabric of every created thing to long for mankind to fulfill their destiny and wholly become the image and likeness of God.

In Genesis 1:20-25, God made sea and air animals before He made land animals, and He made land animals before He made man. He saw that all of them were good. He blessed the animals and commanded them to fill the earth and the seas. He gave Adam the job of caring for them, naming and classifying them. God cares for animals and wants us to care for them as well. As part of the fourth commandment in Deuteronomy 5:17, "Keep the sabbath day." God commanded that we give our animals a rest on the sabbath, just like we give ourselves. They get a full day off every week. Similarly, animals benefited from the sabbatical year. (Leviticus 25) God is very good to animals and to people.

Deuteronomy 22:4 is another scripture that shows God's attention to animals. "Thou shalt not see thy brother's ass or his ox fall down by the way, and hide thyself from them: thou shalt surely help him to lift them up again." Continuing with Deuteronomy 22:6-7, God then forbids the near or full wiping out of an animal species. If someone kills the young, he may not kill the dam or mother. Mom and Dad need to survive to rebuild the species. According to verse seven, our own lives are interconnected with theirs. To go beyond this conservation measure threatens our own wellbeing and affects our longevity. This law alone could have prevented the decimation of sperm whales 200 years ago. "A righteous man regardeth the life of his beast." (Proverbs 12:10)

Psalm 104 is a beautiful song about creation, especially animals, serving God and seeking Him. When they seek God,

He provides for them, and gives them time and space for fun and relaxation.

"²⁴ O Lord, how manifold are thy works! in wisdom hast thou made them all: the earth is full of thy riches.

²⁵ So is this great and wide sea, wherein are things creeping innumerable, both small and great beasts.

²⁶ There go the ships: there is that leviathan, whom thou hast made to play therein.

²⁷ These wait all upon thee; that thou mayest give them their meat in due season."

How do animals wait upon God? In Jonah 3:8, animals do intensified prayer along with the people; with fasting, lying in sackcloth, crying mightily to God and turning from their wicked ways. The prophet Joel forecasted, "The beasts of the field cry also unto thee: for the rivers of waters are dried up, and the fire hath devoured the pastures of the wilderness." (Joel 1:20) Psalm 104:21 says that lions "seek their meat from God." Animals have a spiritual capacity. They know who God is and how to reach Him.

Having seen so many animals doing God's work in Scripture, let's go back to Jonah's whale, who highlights the intelligence of animals. God didn't have to explain his duty to the whale; He only spoke and the whale acted quickly. The whale participated in revival for Jonah and for Nineveh. If he had not swallowed the Hebrew prophet, he would have had a swift death by drowning. If the whale had not vomited out Jonah on land, he would never have reached Nineveh. In fact, Jonah's whale can be seen as a turning point in history, not only for Jonah himself but for the sailors aboard the ship to Tarshish, and for the great city of Nineveh, and for a forecast of the conversion of the Gentile nations to Christ.

Let's finish the Book of Jonah by reading Chapters 3 and 4.

3:1 And the word of the Lord came unto Jonah the second time, saying,

² Arise, go unto Nineveh, that great city, and preach unto it the preaching that I bid thee.

³ So Jonah arose, and went unto Nineveh, according to the word of the Lord. Now Nineveh was an exceeding great city of three days' journey.

⁴ And Jonah began to enter into the city a day's journey, and he cried, and said, Yet forty days, and Nineveh shall be overthrown.

⁵ So the people of Nineveh believed God, and proclaimed a fast, and put on sackcloth, from the greatest of them even to the least of them.

⁶ For word came unto the king of Nineveh, and he arose from his throne, and he laid his robe from him, and covered him with sackcloth, and sat in ashes.

⁷ And he caused it to be proclaimed and published through Nineveh by the decree of the king and his nobles, saying, Let neither man nor beast, herd nor flock, taste any thing: let them not feed, nor drink water:

⁸ But let man and beast be covered with sackcloth, and cry mightily unto God: yea, let them turn every one from his evil way, and from the violence that is in their hands.

⁹ Who can tell if God will turn and repent, and turn away from his fierce anger, that we perish not?

¹⁰ And God saw their works, that they turned from their evil way; and God repented of the evil, that he had said that he would do unto them; and he did it not.

4:1 But it displeased Jonah exceedingly, and he was very angry.

² And he prayed unto the Lord, and said, I pray thee, O Lord, was not this my saying, when I was yet in my country? Therefore I fled before unto Tarshish: for I knew that thou art a gracious God, and merciful, slow to anger, and of great kindness, and repentest thee of the evil.

³ Therefore now, O Lord, take, I beseech thee, my life from me; for it is better for me to die than to live.

⁴ Then said the Lord, Doest thou well to be angry?

⁵ So Jonah went out of the city, and sat on the east side of the city, and there made him a booth, and sat under it in the shadow, till he might see what would become of the city.

⁶ And the Lord God prepared a gourd, and made it to come up over Jonah, that it might be a shadow over his head, to deliver him from his grief. So Jonah was exceeding glad of the gourd.

⁷ But God prepared a worm when the morning rose the next day, and it smote the gourd that it withered.

⁸ And it came to pass, when the sun did arise, that God prepared a vehement east wind; and the sun beat upon the head of Jonah, that he fainted, and wished in himself to die, and said, It is better for me to die than to live.

⁹ And God said to Jonah, Doest thou well to be angry for the gourd? And he said, I do well to be angry, even unto death.

¹⁰ Then said the Lord, Thou hast had pity on the gourd, for the which thou hast not laboured, neither madest it grow; which came up in a night, and perished in a night:

¹¹ And should not I spare Nineveh, that great city, wherein are more than sixscore thousand persons that cannot discern between their right hand and their left hand; and also much cattle?

How do we account for so many perfectly-timed events in Jonah's life and book? Like the deep sleep Jonah had during the storm on the sea. Or, given all the people on the ship, that the casting of lots accurately uncovered Jonah's guilt. Or the whale showing up just in time to save him from drowning. Or the marvelous faith and repentance of Nineveh at Jonah's preaching in Chapter 3. Or the remarkable growth of the gourd (weed) to shade him from the very hot sun (4:6).

God is directly involved in day-to-day events. He guided the actions for the salvation of Nineveh and the preservation of His prophet and his book.

Looking at our own lives, how do we account for well-timed assistance that affected our longevity or our success or failure? Could it be God being kind to us? Perhaps He is seeking our revival, not our destruction. Romans 2:4 says "the goodness of God leadeth thee to repentance." Repentance is how we receive Christ, obtain forgiveness, and prepare for heaven. It is God's kindness and grace to us. (See Acts 3:19.) Psalm 80 indicates that repentance is something God gives us, or does to us. It is the way He turns us from sin to Christ.

2,000 years ago, the early Christian symbol of Jesus was a fish. During early persecutions it was a secret sign among Christians, used to recognize one another and to keep themselves alive and informed. One Christian would draw half of the fish, while the other would draw the rest. It was also used as a password so they could attend worship services. For the safety of their community, without completing the fish drawing one could not gain entrance. A Greek acronym for Jesus in the New Testament is the Greek word for fish: that is, IXTHUS (pronounced Ik'thūs), which stands for "Jesus Christ, God the Son, Savior." Pisces, the two fish in the zodiac, was interpreted by the magi as the ancient symbol of the Church, or the body of Christ. The ancient symbol for the resurrection of the dead and of revival was a dolphin leaping.

In the sky lore of the old magi, this constellation was called Delphinus, as it still is called today. Dolphins are whales.

Jonah ran from God, and the whale was God's messenger of wrath and of mercy. He succeeded in turning Jonah back to obedience to God. Turning from evil deeds to Jesus Christ calls off the whale, or judgment and hell on oneself. This is the whale's message in the Book of Jonah. Just as a great whale can be a sign of impending judgment and a great revival in 760 BC, a great whale can be a sign of both judgment and revival today. Therefore, when we see sperm whales leaping or playing before us, that can be a sign of revival among men, and of people being spiritually resurrected from the dead. Have these things happened to you? Have you repented of your sins and been forgiven and justified through faith in Jesus Christ? Why don't you ask for these blessings from Christ right now, in faith? "Behold now is the accepted time. Behold now is the day of salvation." 2 Corinthians 6:2.

CPSIA information can be obtained
at www.ICGtesting.com
Printed in the USA
BVHW032012270223
659328BV00002B/30